WICKED IDOL

BECKER GRAY

dangerouspress

Wicked Idol
Dangerous Press
Becker Gray © 2020

WICKED IDOL

The new girl doesn't belong here. So why can't I stop thinking about her? Iris Briggs a goodie two-shoes with a headmaster father who aims to ruin my school year before it's even begun. She gets under my skin. With her demure skirts and braided hair, Iris flits around the periphery until she runs right into me, hot coffee soaking me as she looks up at me with wide, innocent eyes. We start off scalding. In the library, we reach lava levels. And then in the city? We go nuclear. She's a good girl, but I'm a Constantine. My duty is to my family. At least, it was until I started unbraiding the good girl and realizing there's more to life than duty.

1

*T*he very first thing I did as a student at Pembroke Preparatory Academy was piss off the Hellfire Club.

It had been an accident—the kind of accident that was entirely preventable, but an accident, nonetheless. I was checking my bag as I walked through the stone-paved courtyard to make sure I'd packed my camera, and then I stumbled right into a bleary-eyed teacher. Not wanting to make any extra enemies among the staff—my father was the new headmaster and had already threatened all the teachers with salary freezes along with promising to gut the athletic department—I staggered sideways and stammered out an apology.

And slammed right into the back of Keaton Constantine, sending his whipped dalgona coffee flying all over the tailored school blazers and silk school ties of his friends.

Not that I knew then that he was *the* Keaton Constantine, rugby captain, king of the school, and scion of one of the most powerful families in New York.

All I knew was that when he wheeled around, he had the fullest, firmest lips and bluest eyes I'd ever seen.

"God, I'm so sorry—" I blurted out, but he cut me off.

"Who the fuck are you?" His eyes raked over me like hot sapphires, taking in my scuffed, secondhand Mary Janes and my brand-new Pembroke uniform.

Which is when I knew I was toast. His derision was obvious in his cruel smirk.

I'd followed the regulations in the student handbook exactly and kept the pleated gray skirt at knee length and wore the sweater embroidered with the Pembroke crest over my white button-up shirt. My red hair was in two simple braids, and I hadn't worn any makeup. I didn't want to draw any attention to myself by flouting the school rules—not to mention my father would've had a fit if his daughter wasn't the paragon of student handbook adherence.

Turns out that I was drawing *more* attention to myself by wearing the uniform perfectly. The other girls had their skirts hemmed up high, fluttering well above their knees, and their shirts untucked and rumpled. Some were clearly in their boyfriend's sweater or blazer, others had skipped it all together, and all of them had artfully messy hair and influencer-level makeup.

The boys were just as bad. Untucked shirts, loosened ties, tousled hair. Some were smoking, others had girls parked on their laps.

And the boys I'd just inadvertently splattered coffee all over were the most insolently rakish of them all.

No, all I'd done with my immaculate and prudish uniform was prove how insignificant I was going to be in the Pembroke Prep social ecosystem. I'd also unofficially stamped myself as little miss uptight with my regulation-to-a-T uniform.

"I said," repeated the boy I'd run into, "*who are you?*" He took a step towards me, dark blond hair tumbling over his forehead. His skin was lightly kissed by the sun, like he'd spent the summer in the Hamptons.

"Um," I said, and then wanted to kick myself. All I wanted was to get through this year alive and get away from my parents. And in order to do that, I needed to survive everything Pembroke Prep would throw at me, including angry boys. "Iris Briggs."

"Briggs," repeated the boy. His eyebrows lifted, highlighting those deep blue eyes. "Like the new Headmaster Briggs? The same new headmaster who is talking about decreasing funding to the athletic department?"

His friends, who'd been busy scowling and disgustedly trying to swipe the coffee off their uniforms, now watched with undisguised interest.

"Perhaps she could send a message to her father for you, Keaton," someone behind him said. I looked past Keaton to see a pale, beautiful boy with glittering onyx eyes and a cruel mouth.

Danger, my mind warned. *That one is dangerous.*

Not that Keaton *wasn't* dangerous—a fact that became clearer as he took another step towards me. He worked his square jaw ever so slightly to the side, and his eyebrows were slashes of irritation over those hypnotic eyes.

And he was big—*jock* big. Tall and broad-shouldered, with muscles that tested the fitted seams of his blazer.

"Listen here, Iris Briggs," he said in a voice full of soft menace. "I'm not going to forget the coffee. And I'm not going to forget what your father is doing. And I'm not going to forget *you*."

He was so close now that he could lean down and kiss me if he wanted. Close enough that I could see the faint crease in his full lower lip.

Stop it. You don't need this kind of trouble.

Shivers raced down my spine, and chills crawled up my neck—even as indignation fired my blood—and something went tight. Low, low in my belly.

I parted my lips—I didn't know what I was going to say, but it was probably going to be something along the lines of *fuck off, dude, it was an accident*—and his eyes dropped down to my mouth. For a minute—an instant —I could swear I saw hunger flash in his stare.

But what he was hungry for? I never found out, because a girl's voice cut into the moment and brought me back to reality.

"Don't worry, sweetheart. He's going to forget you. I'll make sure of it."

I turned around to see a slender girl with dark brown skin, a thick mass of gorgeous curls and big, arty glasses perched on her nose striding towards us. She planted her feet and folded her arms when she got to Keaton. "Fuck off," she told him. "Feeding time is over."

"Yeah, well just so you know, because of her, coffee time is over," one of the other boys said dryly, still mopping at his tie.

"I'm sorry," I said, trying not to sound irritated. But really, it wasn't like I did it on purpose. "I ran into someone else, and I—"

The girl held up a hand to stop me. "Never concede anything to these jackasses. It won't get you anywhere but under their feet."

"You never know until you try, Serafina," the onyx-eyed boy said in a silky voice.

Serafina slid her gaze to him, her eyes narrowing. "How about you try this, Rhys?" And she flipped him off as she looped her free arm through mine and marched me away from the boys.

When I dared to look back, Rhys and the others had clustered back into a circle, muttering to each other and trying to fix their uniforms. But Keaton still stood in the middle of the courtyard, his long fingers curled around his now-empty coffee cup and his furious gaze trained right on me.

***

A few minutes later, we were up the shallow steps and into the main heart of Pembroke, walking into the dim, wood-paneled hallway and stopping by a large window. Through it, I could make out the rolling lawn and the thick Vermont woods clustered around the brick and stone buildings that made up the boarding school. This early in September, everything was still green and sunny and warm, and students were stretched out on the lawn, making out or reading before class.

"I'm Serafina van Doren, by the way," the girl said, by way of introduction. "And you must be Iris Briggs."

"How did you—"

"Rumors have been flying about you," she said, anticipating my question. "We don't get many new students here at Pembroke. Most of us have known each other for years, grown up together and all that. It gets very stale and incestuous, so it's exciting to see a new face."

I could think of five people who weren't excited to meet me. "Who were they?" I asked, pointing my head back towards the courtyard.

"Oh, them?" She twisted her mouth. "They call themselves the Hellfire Club."

The Hellfire Club.

"That's very poetic," I commented.

"It's very ridiculous," Serafina said, rolling her eyes. "But I'd still steer clear of them for a while. They're . . . influential." She said it in the voice of someone reluctantly admitting an indisputable truth.

"Are they dangerous?"

Serafina lifted a shoulder. "Yeah. But just avoid them and you'll be okay. They're like male lions—too lazy to chase anything unless it's threatening their territory."

I thought of Keaton's eyes—sharp and hungry in the morning sunlight. Did he think my father was invading his territory? Or worse, that *I* was?

I looked over my shoulder, suddenly terrified I'd find him at the end of the corridor, watching me.

Serafina sensed my uneasiness and touched my shoulder. "Hey, I promise they won't hurt you, okay? I won't let them. They're mostly harmless. Well, except for Lennox Lincoln-Ward, the boy with the white hair; his only goal in life is to torture Sloane."

"Sloane?"

"My roommate. She's very quiet, a little scary, but she keeps to herself mostly. I don't know why Lennox hates her so much—well, other than that he's an asshole."

I think of the boy behind Keaton, the one with the glittering eyes and sharp mouth. "What about the one you called Rhys?"

Serafina frowned. "Okay, maybe I lied about them being harmless. If the Hellfire Club were all lions, Rhys would be the lion who kills for fun. He would be Uncle Scar. Be careful around him."

"And Keaton? Should I be careful around him too?"

Serafina hesitated, then shook her head. "No. Like I said, just avoid him and he'll forget about you. Constantines are like that."

"Constantines?"

Serafina tilted her head. "You really are new, aren't you? The Constantine family is like the Kennedys—if the Kennedys made their money doing shady shit. Oh and owned half of New York City."

"Half?"

"I mean, I'm including the legal holdings as well as the less-than-legal holdings here."

Alarm spiked. "Um, are they like a *crime* family?"

"Only in the technical sense," Serafina said, waving a hand, like I was getting hung up on some insignificant detail. "They're very respectable otherwise. One of those Mayflower families, you know, like all the women wear real pearls, every summer is spent in Bishop's Landing, they go golfing in Kiawah, that kind of thing."

A *respectable* crime family? That didn't seem like a thing to me. "I'm less worried about their respectability than I am Keaton having me whacked or something."

Serafina burst into giggles. "Whacked?"

"Whacked! Offed! Rolled into a tarp and then fed to the local deer or whatever!"

She was still laughing. "I promise the Constantines don't feed people to deer. And don't worry about Keaton. He really will forget all about this morning; he's usually too busy with his girlfriend and rugby to worry about anything else. And anyway, you're with me now."

"I am?"

"You are," she confirmed, beaming at me. "I'm the queen around here. And Sloane is my lady knight. We'll make sure none of those Hellfire morons bother you."

Relief and gratitude eased something in my chest. "Thank you," I said.

"What class do you have first? I'll walk you there."

I pulled out my schedule. "AP Physics."

"Excellent! Sloane does too." We started walking down the hall towards the south wing of the school, where all the science labs and lecture rooms were. For the first time since my father took this post, I started to feel a little hopeful that this year might not be so terrible after all, even if I had inadvertently angered the son of a *respectable* crime family.

"So, what's it like being the headmaster's daughter?" Serafina asked.

As we walked to the physics lab, other students called out to her or playfully tugged on her blazer or reached out for high fives. She strode through it all like a monarch striding through a throng of courtiers, and I knew she hadn't been joking about being the queen.

I was even more grateful she'd decided to befriend me. If anyone could keep me safe from Keaton's furious stare, it would be her.

"It's mostly terrible," I said. "This is the third school of his I've gone to, and he always wants me to be the best at everything. I used to think he'd go easier on me once I turned eighteen and my perfect older sister moved out, but no. Not to mention he's not really down with my photography obsession."

I didn't elaborate any more than that. I was still upset about my birthday this summer, when I'd announced to him that I wanted to study photography in Paris and not law at an Ivy like he wanted me to. He'd wanted me to be more like Isabelle—the obedient one, the one who did everything right, including getting impeccable grades at LSE.

He'd yelled; I'd yelled back.

My mother had hidden, like she always did whenever there was conflict.

"Photography?" Serafina asked. "That's pretty fucking cool. Are you taking a class on it this year?"

Excitement—real excitement—fizzed in my veins and made me smile. "Yeah. Advanced photography seminar. First class is on Friday."

She smiled back as we got to my classroom. "I've got another lady knight in there. Aurora. She'll make sure you're taken care of."

"You really are the queen here."

"I'm a van Doren," she said, like that explained everything. "Ah, Sloane! Save a seat for Iris, would you?"

I looked across the room to see an unsmiling white girl with a very short, no-nonsense ponytail and a helix piercing high on one ear. When I came up to the table and held out my hand, she shook it without a word. But her green eyes were quick and keen as she took in everything about me, and her handshake was strong and efficient. She seemed like the kind of person who knew where every exit in the room was, along with everything that could be turned into a weapon.

"Sloane, this is Iris. We're adopting her. Also, make sure Keaton leaves her alone."

Sloane nodded and silently gestured for me to take a seat.

Serafina left with a wave and a promise to see me at lunch, and then the physics professor burst into the room, breathless and late, and just like that, my first day at Pembroke Prep had officially started.

Now, it was time to forget about Keaton Constantine. I was going to lay low and survive until Paris, when my life could truly begin, and I didn't have time to worry about spilled coffee or the rugby-playing sons of well-mannered criminals.

And I definitely didn't have the time to think about his full lips and tousled blond hair. Or his wide, powerful shoulders. Or his midnight-blue eyes.

No time at all.

I flipped open a fresh notebook, took a deep breath, and began taking notes.

*B*loody back-to-school night.

I knew for a fact the storied tradition was designed for the purpose of torturing students. The only people who looked forward to the weekend were parents who loved to come back to Pembroke Prep. Show off their money, their influence, all the while leaving behind their precious cargo for someone else to raise, someone else to teach.

Well, most parents anyway. My mother was wholly devoted to her fulltime job of being the matriarch of the Constantine family—which mostly involved hosting lavish parties, keeping my sister Elaine out of the press, and making sure my oldest brother Winston continued raking in money for the family through our various business holdings. She wasn't cold, but she wasn't warm either, and it didn't matter how many rugby games I played or how many championships I won, she was more concerned with my future than my present.

And my dad?

Dead.

Murdered five years ago, killed by the fucking Morellis —not that we could ever prove it.

He would have been here tonight, I thought bitterly. He never missed anything. He was a busy man, certainly, and not always an easy man to love, but he did love us, and we fucking loved him.

And now he was gone, and sometimes it felt like all my mother wanted was for us to forget our own lives and jump right into forwarding his legacy.

But not that you care.

Not that I expected Mom to show up today anyway. After all, I wasn't perfect, successful Winston, or forever-a-mess Elaine. And I wasn't Tinsley, the baby of the family, who'd decided to go to school closer to home in Bishop's Landing. I made a mental note to myself to check in on her later and make sure she was staying well away from trouble.

So, no Mom and gotta babysit Tinsley. Awesome start to the year.

Even *Rhys's* parents were here. And given that Rhys was the devil himself, I was pretty certain he had nothing but disdain for them. It wasn't a stretch; Rhys disdained everyone. If you weren't Hellfire, you were on his shit list. Top of that shit list was Serafina van Doren.

New girl's new best friend.

Stop calling her new girl. You know her name. After all you've been low-key stalking her for the past week and a half.

So sue me if I'd made it a point to know everything there was to know about Little Miss Perfect with the perfect parents. I made it my business to know. After all, I was in line to be valedictorian. If she was a threat, I needed to know that.

Also, I was a Constantine. I might not be my tightly wound oldest brother, but control was still in my blood. She was an unknown quantity and I needed to quantify her, that was all.

Oh sure, those are the only reasons.

My phone buzzed, and I scowled down at it as I headed towards the British literature stacks in the back. Clara . . . again.

Clara: Where are you?

Clara: Can you run interference?

Clara: You okay?

I tried not to be annoyed about my wellbeing being last. After all, Clara was Clara. And she had her own cross to bear. If Caroline Constantine's parenting motto was *rub some dirt on it*, the Blairs' motto was *Mommy and Daddy know best*. Which was why Clara pretended to date me, a Constantine, when she was really going out with a local boy and had been for the past two years. I told her that if the townie knocked her up, she was on her own though. Not because I didn't care about Clara—she was one of my oldest friends—but because Caroline Constantine would kill us both . . . after the baby was born and she'd already whisked it off to Bishop's Landing to play with bespoke silver rattles while wearing the same booties as the royal babies did or whatever.

I slid my phone back into my pocket without answering.

I couldn't be bothered with Clara or her helicopter parents right now. The last thing I wanted to do was have to explain why my mother couldn't be bothered to visit while I mustered up dry cheek-kisses and hugs to keep up the ruse that Clara and I were truly together.

The library, on the other hand, was safe. It was the first stop on back-to-school night. The headmaster always gave his address here, and Headmaster Briggs had already finished his pointless speech and then whisked the parents off to see the new swimming pool, which left my Pembroke sanctuary completely to me. Which meant I could lose myself in Keats and Longfellow as I waited for the wealthy and elite and the sycophantic to give me my campus back.

Amongst the stacks and stacks of books and the nooks and crannies, I'd learned to find solace. A little peace and quiet where no one would look for me. Sometimes, it was like they all thought I was a jock only and forgot that I was smart. And actually liked to read.

As I strolled along the smooth stone tile at the library, surrounded by the dark wood and stacks of books at the reference section, I inhaled it all. That smell of vellum and leather. It always brought a smile to my face.

Books helped me get out of my own head when my family was being waspish dicks, which was pretty much every damn day. Luckily, aside from Tinsley, I didn't have to deal with them today.

I passed one of the stacks and paused, then took a quick sniff. *What was that smell?*

It smelled like something floral. Something sweet. It smelled like *her*.

The new girl.

Fucking Iris Briggs.

I'd gotten close enough to her that first day to catch a hint of roses and vanilla in the air. It wasn't overwhelming like some girls who liked to drown themselves in the latest Dior or Lady Gaga, or God help them, eau de RiRi.

No. This was some simple essential oil type of shit. Just enough to linger and tease. Not enough to overpower. But she wasn't here.

As a matter of fact, I'd barely seen her since that first day. It was almost like she was taking all routes to purposely avoid me.

Why do you care? You have Clara.

Yes, I did have Clara. At least, that's what everyone believed. We were the golden couple, the ones people wanted to be like. I wondered how people would really feel if they found out just how fucked up Clara and I both were.

Well, they're never going to figure that out.

When I turned towards the fiction stacks, I froze. There, perched on one of the rolling ladders, was the source of the rose and vanilla. The source of my fucking sleepless nights for the past week. "What the fuck are you doing here?"

Her head snapped up and she gasped. "Jesus, you scared the shit out of me."

Why was she looking at me like that? All fresh faced with her sky-blue eyes and her dusting of freckles on display and looking so clean and fresh and fucking pure. I wanted to make her dirty.

What the fuck is wrong with you?

"I repeat. What the hell are you doing here?"

She narrowed her eyes. "It's a free country," she said slowly, as if she was trying to control her temper. "I'm reading. What are *you* doing in here?"

I scowled. Maybe no one had told her how things worked here. I asked the questions. New girl provided the answers. That's how it was supposed to go.

"Don't you know it's back-to-school night?"

The narrowed eyes turned into a full-fledged scowl. She lifted a brow. "You might remember my father is the headmaster? I don't need to be there for back-to-school night."

"Well, then, does your father know you're here?"

There, in her eyes, that quick shift of her gaze, and then the slamming shut of the book. "Look, this library is enormous. We can both find corners and avoid each other, right?"

"Oh no, if you look, the library is really only big enough for one of us."

"Well, I'm not leaving. So you can either get used to that idea or find somewhere else to hide."

"Who said I was hiding?" Why did she see so damn much?

"Come on, everyone else is with their parents, having fun, taking a break from classes, introducing their friends, introducing their teachers. You're skulking around the library with me. You already know I'm avoiding my parents. Why are *you* avoiding yours?"

I studied her. She wasn't beautiful. Not in the ordinary sense of the word. But she was striking, completely engaging. From her bright red hair to those blue eyes. The dusting of freckles on her nose. Her straight, even, white teeth to that complete doll bow of a mouth. A bottom lip plump enough to make me want to bite it.

"You know those pigtail things make you look like you're twelve."

She frowned at that. "That the best you got? I asked you a question."

I shrugged. "You're in my hiding spot. I'm not really one for the whole parental love fest." Also . . . neither was my mother.

"I didn't see your name on it. It's a library. Everyone is welcome to come and read books."

What was it about her that irritated me so much? I didn't like that she was in my space. I didn't like that she'd taken my sanctuary. I didn't like that she so casually stood here, wrecking the only peace and quiet I knew I was going to find today.

I didn't like *her*, period. "You have ten minutes to find your book and get out."

She hopped down from the ladder, placing one of the books on the ground on her neat little stack of other books. "Oh, I think I'll stay."

"I think you didn't hear me."

She tilted her chin up. "Oh, I heard you. I just don't care. I've looked and looked, but I can't seem to find a fuck to give about your opinion."

I don't know what possessed me, but I boxed her in, causing her to back up against the books. "You are a mouthy little thing, aren't you?" I reached out a finger and toyed with a stray tendril of hair. "What I'm curious about is what would make the headmaster's daughter hide."

"I don't think you'd get it if I told you. Besides, you don't get something for nothing. I tell you, you tell me."

"That's not how this works."

"Oh my god, you're so full of yourself."

"Tell me something I don't know." Somehow, fighting with this girl made my skin tingle. I could feel it reverberating from my toes to the top of my head. She was irritating. A complete klutz. Mouthy. I didn't like that at all.

My dick was eager as ever to disagree with me. He and I were currently not on speaking terms as every time I thought about Iris, he got hard. Like a moron. "I don't think I like you very much."

She tilted her chin and smiled up at me, completely unafraid. Her gaze locked on mine, too direct, seeing more than I wanted her to. I planted both hands on either side of her head. "Tell me why you're hiding in here."

"Like I said, *you first.*"

Her tongue peeked out to lick her bottom lip, and I bit back a groan.

What the fuck was that?

I wanted to go and slide up to that flame that sparked around her, like a clueless moth, flapping to my death. And when she licked her lips again, I forgot all about why I shouldn't do this or how stupid it would be if I did.

Nope. Instead, I just leaned in and kissed her.

She tasted like strawberries. Sweet, with a little chaser of sharp tang. When she parted her lips in a gasp, I deepened the kiss. Licking into her mouth. Desperate to taste what I could before this all ended.

But still, a part of me waited. I waited for her to push me away. I waited for her to tell me to stop. *I* waited for that signal.

I *wanted* that signal. I wanted her to set that line I would not cross. But, instead, she let me kiss her.

Even better, or worse, depending on how you looked at it, she kissed me back.

I angled my head with a groan, dipping my knees slightly so I could capture her mouth better. She was so small in comparison to me.

My tongue stroked over hers, darting and playing and sliding. She further tortured me by making this meowing sound at the back of her throat. Did she know that it made me want to take up residence right fucking here and never leave?

The sound was part whimper, part moan, and all mine. It was the kind of kiss that was full of promise. Still, warning bells rang in the back of my mind because I should not be kissing this girl. I did not have time for this shit.

Hell, I didn't even *like* this girl.

Uh-huh, keep telling yourself that.

Despite myself telling my brain not to give in to the command, my hands slid to her face, and then in her hair. I fought with the braids until they started to unravel. With the silken weight of her hair flooding over my fingers, I cupped her cheeks and a whimper broke. The clash of our tongues sent a shiver with a lava chaser through my veins. I wanted to consume her. I could kiss her forever.

Before I knew what I was doing, she mewled again and arched her back, bringing her hips slightly forward, seeking . . .

I would like to be able to say that this kiss was nothing, that I didn't care, that she was only mildly fuckable, and I was bored with no one better to do. But that little motion told me that she wanted *me . . . me,* not anyone else, *me.*

It meant I could no longer walk away. I could no longer trust my thoughts and actions, because I slid my hands further into her tresses, tightening my grip, and I shook the leashes of control off, kissing her for everything I was worth, making the kiss count for everything with a girl I didn't like.

She was just someone I needed in this moment. Just call her a chaser of bad dreams, because with my lips on hers, I didn't think about the loneliness. I didn't take into account how isolated I felt most of the day. It didn't occur to me to feel unwanted, unloved, because in this moment, this girl who I barely knew, was letting me kiss her and she was kissing me back.

When she rolled her hips again, a growl broke the hushed moans.

Was that me?

It must have been, because I pressed her body into the stacks, my hands sliding down to her waist, then her ass. I picked her up, bracing her against the shelves. Squeezing her ass and holding her the way that I needed so her heat gyrated against my dick.

Fuck. Me.

I felt like the top of my head was going to blow off. Like I'd voluntarily tied myself up with a live wire and I couldn't fucking stop.

What was I doing? I had to think about Clara. This would be bad for the two of us if someone fucking saw.

But Iris wasn't Clara. And something about that made this far hotter.

A loud bang downstairs startled us apart, just enough that she tore her now-plump and bruised lips from mine, but we still shared breath. The startle wasn't enough for me to let her go though. I still held the firm cheeks of her ass in my palms, and I couldn't help another squeeze.

She wasn't like the other girls wearing thongs and skirts so short a brisk wind would tell me who had a carpet or hardwood floors. It was hotter somehow that my hands were on her ass and I was the only one who knew she was rocking bikinis. My blood ran with lava at the idea that her pussy maintenance practices were somehow still a mystery. I loved being the only one even close to knowing.

Her gaze leveled on me as she dragged in sharp pants. This close I could see just how thick and dark her lashes were. Not from any assistance of monthly trips to the esthetician, but because those were simply her lashes.

Iris was purity personified, and I wanted to be the asshole who made her dirty.

Her lips parted like she wanted to say something, but her eyes were glassy, unfocused. Likely a mirror of my own.

That line I'd been waiting for her to draw, she drew it then with a gentle push at my chest, and I eased her down, but not before rocking her once more against my steel-hard dick.

She needed to know what she'd done to me. She needed to own some of that responsibility. When her feet touched the ground, I pushed away from the devil's own temptation and stalked from the library as quickly as my legs would carry me.

3

IRIS

a week later, and I could still feel Keaton Constantine's lips against my own.

His kiss had been hungry. *Angry*. Like he was furious with me for being kissable. Maybe even for being alive.

And his hands—his hands had been everywhere. Taking apart my two braids and sifting through my hair.

Big and rough on my bottom as he lifted me up and rubbed me against him.

And that thing I'd rubbed against . . .

Being the headmaster's daughter meant that I'd missed out on a lot of the usual boarding school experiences. No fooling around after hours, no parties where I could've gotten hot and heavy with a boy. No fumbling sex in a dorm room.

But even I knew what Keaton had been pressing against me in the library. Even I knew that it would be as big and unapologetically male as the rest of him.

Keaton Constantine had been hard for *me*, the headmaster's daughter. He'd wanted more than kissing, and I think I would have given it to him. Anything he wanted, because in that moment, the entire world had shrunk to only us, and there were only lips and tongues and that maddening flicker of heat between my legs. Like someone had lit a sparkler low in my belly.

And then he'd left.

I'd pushed him away to catch my breath, and he'd turned and left me there without another word.

What the *fuck*?

"Earth to Iris," a concerned British voice said, breaking through my thoughts.

I turned to see Aurora Lincoln-Ward staring at me, a delicate eyebrow arched over an unnerving gold-colored eye.

She was Lennox's twin sister, and they were alike in several ways: an accent as a gift from their British father, pale, unearthly features, and an inborn arrogance from having a mother who was a minor Liechtensteiner princess—which made them royalty, too.

Like Lennox, she had bright gold eyes. Like a bird of prey. Or a lioness. Eyes she set off to her advantage by dying her white-blond hair a shade of inky, midnight black.

But unlike her twin, Aurora adored Sloane.

Luckily for me, she was also unlike Lennox in that she hated the Hellfire Club and every single boy in it. So when she'd learned that I'd accidentally pissed them off on my first day, Aurora had sworn me her friendship and protection, just as Sloane and Serafina had.

It was a good feeling. I'd never really had close friends before, not from school at least, and I needed them now more than ever.

I cleared my throat and shifted in my seat, feeling a little squirmy from the memory of Keaton's kiss. "Yeah?"

"I was asking you what this was all about," Aurora said, tugging at a letter sticking out of my notebook. She kept her voice down because our photography seminar had technically started, but the teacher was still at the front fiddling with her laptop and trying to get today's presentation on the screen. "Why is it written in French?"

My face heated—half excitement, half nervousness. "I applied to the Sorbonne for college, and even though I'm still waiting for a formal acceptance letter, they invited me to apply for a pre-degree program there. It starts in November and goes until July, and I'd get to work with the professors and professional photographers in Paris . . . It would mean getting a head start on the other students. Maybe even on my career."

"Sounds amazing," Aurora remarked. "Except that you'll be here at Pembroke that entire time."

"I could graduate right now if I wanted," I said, a little wistfully. "I've got the credits. But . . ."

"But?"

I sighed. "My father doesn't want me to go to Paris or study photography. He wants me to go to Harvard or somewhere like that. Go into law."

Aurora wrinkled her nose. "Good god. Why?"

I gave a cynical laugh. "Because it would be excellent for his career. If he can run a school well enough that one of his kids is an Ivy-educated lawyer on her way to the Supreme Court? If he can show off that *both* his disciplined, grounded daughters are working hard at Very Serious and Important majors? Then what school board wouldn't consider hiring him?"

"The Sorbonne is hardly an unaccredited community college," Aurora pointed out. "It's the oldest university in Europe."

"Oh, I know. But if I'm in Paris, then he can't control my life like he did my sister's, and he hates that. And photography is a joke to him."

"But—"

I didn't find out what Aurora was about to say, because at just that moment, the door to the classroom opened and Keaton Constantine insolently strolled in with his leather bag slung across his chest and his typical arrogant smirk tilting his lips.

He didn't see me at first, which meant I had time to observe how a thick lock of hair had dropped out of its classic, all-American style to drift over his forehead. I had time to see how his tailored school blazer showed off his firm chest and broad shoulders.

I had time to remember how those big hands—which were currently handing Ms. Sanderson a note—felt as they moved through my hair and as they curled around my hips.

My entire body felt like it was on fire.

He gave the classroom a bored once-over as Ms. Sanderson read the note. When his eyes lit on me, his entire body went rigid.

His blue eyes were turbulent—*incensed*—as he narrowed them at me, as if I'd somehow known he would be in this classroom today and had manipulated my entire schedule in order to be here just to annoy him.

"What. A. Bastard," Aurora muttered under her breath, catching his glare at me.

I agreed, and I wasn't having it. Not today. Not after he dropped me in the library and left me like so much forgettable trash.

I glared right back at him.

"Well, welcome to the class, Mr. Constantine," Ms. Sanderson said. "Luckily for you, last week was only an orientation, and so you haven't missed much. Take a seat anywhere, and if I can have you all put down your phones now—yes, thank you—I've got this presentation fired up now, and we can get started."

Ms. Sanderson started talking about representational interpretations versus abstraction as Keaton strode to the back of the classroom, giving me a final glower as he passed my desk.

I was about to breathe a sigh of relief when he dropped into the empty desk right behind mine and propped his shoes against the legs of my chair.

I turned while Ms. Sanderson kept lecturing, keeping my voice in a low hiss. "You know, there're other empty desks if you're so opposed to being near me."

"I'm fine right here," he said softly. Defiantly. His eyes glittered as he spoke.

I turned back around, livid. And a little bit hurt.

We didn't see each other for a week after that kiss, and *this* was how he acted when he saw me again?

Fine.

I guess I knew where things stood then.

"The partnered semester project will involve an interpretation of landscapes," Ms. Sanderson was saying at the front of the room.

I heard a faint, collective murmur of discontent ripple up around me, and Ms. Sanderson held up her hands. "I know, I know, landscapes are boring, but hear me out. The word *interpretation* is key, because I'll be asking you to step outside your comfort zone and add an element of illustration to your images. You will not only have to capture twelve stunning images of your landscape, but then you will have to use art and design to transform these images into something that tells a story. *And* you must do this all collaboratively—the photography and the design are to be a joint effort. I expect both partners to influence the project with their individual perspectives."

I looked over to Aurora, who was already looking over at me. She tilted her head and gave me a smile—the universal signal for *let's do this*.

I'd only just smiled back at her when Ms. Sanderson ruined the moment.

"We're going to pair up alphabetically," she said. "Which means—oh, that's right, Mr. Constantine has joined us. Okay, one minute..." She bent over a stack of folders on the teacher's table at the front of the room, writing on Post-It notes and tapping in notes onto her tablet, then she straightened up after two or three minutes. "All fixed!"

She started to walk up and down the rows of desks as she handed us each a folder. "You'll see your partner's name on the front of your folder. Now, the assignment gives you three weeks to prepare your prospectus, but may I suggest you start working on it now . . ."

Ms. Sanderson's voice faded away as I looked down at the folder on my desk. There, written in Ms. Sanderson's spiky, rushed handwriting, was the last name I ever wanted to see.

Keaton Constantine.

Briggs. Constantine.

Alphabetically close.

Ugh.

My stomach dropped right to the floor—and my heart along with it. I couldn't be his partner, I just couldn't. To have to see him, talk with him, *work* with him . . . In close proximity?

To have to share my photography with him, which was the *one* thing I kept for myself, the one thing that made me happy and the one thing my father couldn't control . . .

No. I couldn't do it. Not when Keaton was so cruel, so angry. Not when he could kiss me like he did and then just walk away like it meant nothing.

I didn't turn around to see what Keaton's reaction to this was, but I didn't have to. He leaned forward and said in a low voice I could barely hear, "Guess it's a good thing I joined the class when I did. *Partner*." He sounded utterly furious.

"You may spend this time getting acquainted with your collaborator and discussing plans for your project," Ms. Sanderson announced, reaching the front of the room and sitting at her desk, presumably to spend the next twenty minutes surreptitiously updating her resume.

I spun around immediately and gave Keaton my fiercest glare. "This might be a blow-off class for you, Mr. Rugby Captain, but this is important to me. You may rule the school, but you don't rule *me*, and especially not when it comes to this project. Got it?"

He blinked once, like I'd surprised him, and then a slow, cocky grin slid over his face.

And God help me, when he smiled like that, I could have gone up in flames.

Because when Keaton scowled, he was sexy as hell, but when he *smiled*?

It was like a fallen angel had come to claim my heart.

"You're afraid of me," he said confidently. "That's what this is."

"I'm not afr—that's ridiculous—" Who the hell did he think he was?

He nodded, stroking his jaw in mock-thoughtfulness. "You're afraid that if we work together, you won't be able to keep from kissing me again."

"*Again?*" I sputtered. "You kissed *me*! Remember?" The arrogant...insufferable...egotistical...jackass had another think coming. I wasn't kissing him again.

Aurora looked over at him, her gaze murderous. I realized I'd been talking a little loudly, so I lowered my voice after giving her a quick *all clear* smile. "Remember? I was minding my own business, and then you leaned in and kissed me. I had nothing to do with it."

He leaned forward over his desk, his smile fading into something darker. More intense. "Nothing to do with it? So that wasn't you licking your lips while you stared at my mouth? That wasn't you purring into my kiss as I helped you grind against my cock?"

I flushed so bright that I knew my cheeks probably matched my hair. I could feel the beads of sweat forming on my skin as my temperature reached peak embarrassment levels.

"That's what I thought," he said, sitting back. His voice held a note of satisfaction, but there was a predatory glint to his eyes that was anything but satisfied.

"Well, it's not going to happen again," I said sharply. No way was I going to be that vulnerable—that *needy* —again, and then watch him walk away. *Again.*

"Fine by me, Miss Perfect," Keaton snapped. The scowl was back in full force again, like whatever I'd said had displeased him. Which couldn't be true—I didn't have that kind of power over him. And he had a girlfriend anyway. *And* he hated me.

"So now that that's out of the way, should we get started?" My voice was still sharp, and I kept my face down so he couldn't see my eyes. So he couldn't see all the stupid hope and hurt there.

"Fine then," he drawled. He gave his pen a contemptuous click and then flipped open his folder. "Let's get fucking started."

"*Y*ou want to get drinks? Phineas is in one of his moods, and I can't handle it without a properly made martini."

I shook my head at Owen. "Can't." I held up my phone and waggled it. "Monthly penance."

Owen winced.

He was probably my closest friend in the Hellfire Club —which, might I add, was a dumb name for us, but I hadn't started it, so who was I to judge? At any rate, as my closest friend, Owen was the only one who knew how complicated the Constantines really were. And like any good friend, he kept his mouth shut and didn't say too much. But I had a feeling that later today, I'd find a bottle of Don Q Reserva Rum in my room.

No note or explanation, just one friend saying to another: God, life sucks. Here is this insanely expensive bottle of rum with which to chase that shit away.

I was a senior, so I'd earned the right to one of the coveted corner single rooms with its own shower. The rooms were passed down from seniors to those deserving. My friends and I had begged, borrowed, stolen, and forged to have these rooms. But it was well worth it to not have anyone around for the shit show that was about to take place.

After the shower, I grabbed my sports drink from my fridge, tossed myself onto my bed, and prepared for hell.

Outside the window, something caught my eye, sinking my already dour mood and making my lips turn down. There she was . . . *fucking Iris.* The reason I'd taken to two-a-day spank sessions.

Didn't matter how much I drank or worked out; I could *still* taste her. I could practically feel her under my skin. *And you want more.*

My situation wasn't entirely my fault though. She'd been there in my space with her smart mouth and her fucking freckles and I'd just . . . lost it. With irritation, I glanced down and realized I was hard. *Goddamn it.*

What the hell was it about that girl?

You better figure it out because you're going to be trapped with her for months.

Fucking hell.

Tomorrow, I would see if Ms. Sanderson would pair me with someone else. While my mother seemed to think the only thing I was good for was eventually filling a suit at one of Winston's offices, I was damn good at multimedia and design. If I wanted, I could go to college and study it. Design was nothing that would make her proud though, which meant I still hadn't made up my mind what I was going to do after I graduated. It was dumb—because I did still want to make her proud—but the idea of working for Winston . . . working for the family . . .

Ugh.

Either way, no matter what I ended up choosing, I was not going to have my opportunities tainted by some no-name girl.

I dragged my eyes away from her because all she was, was a fucking distraction. And she wasn't even that hot.

Then why are we hard?

My dick twitched as if to argue the fact. But what the hell did he know? I deliberately pulled my blinds down so I wouldn't be tempted to look out on the lawn at her, Serafina, and Sloane enjoying the sunny day.

Instead, I turned my attention to my phone, hit the speed dial, and waited. Sometimes I had to call twice because my mother forgot. This was not one of those days though, thankfully. But my mother still sounded confused. "Keaton?"

"Yes, Mother, you know, your son? Sadly, we have a standing date, same time every second Saturday of the month."

She gave me an exasperated sigh. "Of course I know we have a standing call. I have just been busy, that's all." Each word was laced with something too well-mannered to be overt irritation, but too clipped to be true politeness. "Well, are you fine?"

"Yeah, Mom. Just fine."

"Keaton, there is no reason for the attitude."

I sighed. I should have been used to this. The way she spoke to me as if I was a chart of statistics. "Classes are going well. Straight As. Top of the class. No problems. Rugby is fine. We have a pre-season match against

Croft Wells Academy in a few weeks, and I was hoping you could attend."

She sighed. "I'd love to, but I've got too much on my plate with the gala. You know how it is."

I swallowed the bite of irritation. I did know how it was, and I hated it. The Constantine Foundation was one of my mother's pet projects, and every year they hosted a massive gala to raise money for whatever the charity du jour was. It took months to plan, and then all that hard work was wasted on four boozy hours in a boutique art museum.

"Well, if that's all, I'll just hop off the phone then."

A *tsk*. "I do not understand why you have to be like this. It's just busy here. One day you'll be home, working for the family like Winston is, and then you'll see."

I waited for it. The weight of disappointment. The guilt of not being like Winston—driven and ambitious and controlled.

I didn't feel it today though. After all these years, I'd finally become numb to it.

When I was younger and Dad was alive, Mom had spent more time with me—at least, that's how I'd remembered it. But as I got older, she distanced herself. Not cruelly, not coldly, nothing like that. But just like I was a scotch that hadn't finished distilling yet, a cake that hadn't finished baking. Which was her prerogative, I guess. After all, what the fuck did I care? I'd be free in a year. I could go wherever and do whatever I wanted, and nobody would give a fuck.

I was a Constantine and the world would be mine for the taking, whether I did what my family wanted or not.

For some inexplicable reason, my gaze darted to my pulled blinds, and I tugged them open because I had to know what Iris was doing. Glutton for punishment. It had to be the call with my mother. I might as well distract myself. And Little Miss Perfect was going to have to do for now.

My mother was still talking about how busy she was and how I had to understand, when she called my name. "Keaton?"

"Mom."

"I really do wish I could come to your game, you know." I could hear her trying to think of the next conciliatory thing to say. "Has there been any more interest from scouts?"

"Coach says yes. But I won't know more until the preseason games get closer."

"Are you still thinking about . . . doing it professionally?"

It had been a fight when I'd first brought up the possibility at a memorable family dinner a couple years ago. She wanted me working for Winston, *period*. Married well, *period*.

In her eyes, none of that would happen if I was travelling the world playing a sport with common people.

But despite what everyone else assumed about a Constantine kid, I didn't want to spend my days doing fuck-all nothing in a suit, handshaking and moving money around. I needed purpose. Something to do. A reason for existing. And if I didn't do design, then going pro with rugby wouldn't be the worst thing, right? Binding myself to some kind of family, artificial though it may be?

But do I really want to play rugby for the rest of my life...?

"I haven't made any decisions yet," I told her honestly.

"Good." She sounded relieved. "And your cousin Cash? Have you checked in with him?"

Cash was a lanky sophomore with great hair and no sense of self-preservation, which I deduced from his immediate attraction to Sloane Lauder—who was basically a knife in the shape of a human girl.

And for better or for worse, he was also my cousin.

"Cash is fine," I told her. "Same as last year. Not getting into any trouble." *Yet.*

"Good," Mom said. And then paused. "So . . ."

Oh god. *Here it comes.*

"Are things with Clara going well?"

"Fine."

Maybe less fine ever since you shoved your tongue in Iris's mouth.

That had been like a week ago. I hadn't done it again, so maybe I wasn't a shitty pseudo-cheater. "But I've been thinking."

She was quiet for a breath. "What do you mean?"

"Clara's a great girl, but it's not like we're getting married or anything. She's very sweet. I care about her a lot. But I don't really think that there's a point in continuing to date her."

"Keaton Constantine, what the hell?"

My brows popped. My mother rarely swore. "Wow, Mom. I didn't even know you knew that word."

"That relationship is important," Mom explained, sounding like she was struggling for patience. "It's your future."

"Mom, I'm eighteen. You can't really expect me to date the same girl for the rest of my life."

"I can, and I do. You've been raised together. *Groomed* to be together. It's not like you need to get to know her. You know exactly what kind of family she comes from. You should know that the expectation is that you two will get married."

I laughed at that. "Again, we're eighteen. We're not going to marry *anyone* any time soon. And while I care about her, I don't love her."

I could envision her pinched face. "You're being very naïve," my mother said in a brittle voice. "Constantines marry well. That's what we do. And it's your role in the family to connect us with the Blairs."

"And if I don't want to?"

Mom didn't say anything for a second. "Keaton, don't make me compel you."

"With money?" That was, after all, my parents' go-to move.

She didn't answer, but she didn't need to. I had a trust fund and a monthly allowance that would balance the budgets of most Midwestern states—but both of those could be fucked with. By her. The first wave of trust fund money would be released once I graduated—and it would be enough to see me through college until I could get my own job . . . if I didn't choose a career in rugby, that was. If I chose rugby, I'd need fuck-all from the family.

But again, I couldn't start playing pro until after graduation at the soonest.

"You're telling me that if I don't keep dating Clara, you're going to starve me out financially?"

"Don't be gauche," she said. She disliked overt money talk. "I'm just reminding you that the benefits of this family are tied to *service* to this family."

"Does it matter to you that Clara doesn't love me? Never mind how *I* feel?"

"This isn't about love, sweetheart, this is about a merger of the families. Something better and stronger. You'll see."

I ground my teeth together. My gaze went outside my window again.

To Iris.

My skin was too hot and too prickly as I remembered the slide of her tongue over mine, that sound she made at the back of her throat, the way her ass fit my hands when I lifted her against me.

And fantastic. I had to stop. *Fuck.* Why *that* girl? I didn't have time for that shit.

"Keaton? Are you listening to me?"

I dragged my attention back to my conversation. "Sorry, I was paying attention to a project I need to focus on. What did you say?"

"I told you, nurture that relationship. Please don't disappoint me. The Blairs are some of my closest friends and could be our strongest allies."

"Whatever you say. Are we done here? Can I go?"

"Keaton," Mom said, and then paused. When she spoke again, her voice was gentler. "I'm trying to raise you as your father would have wanted. I'm trying to steer this family the way your father would have wanted. That's all."

My heart stuttered at the mention of Dad, at the giant Lane-Constantine-shaped hole in all of our lives.

"Okay," I said finally.

"Okay. I love you, sweetheart."

"Yeah, love you too," I choked out and hung up the phone. I swallowed the pain as my eyes stayed fixed on Little Miss Perfect's ass.

I hadn't focused on my anger. It was *her*. *She* was near. Why would I even be thinking about breaking up with Clara? That kiss wouldn't have happened. I could have just skated through senior year with no waves made, my mom none the wiser about me and Clara. Then I'd be the hell out of here and could do what I wanted.

But Iris was the reason for this. *She* was the reason I was thinking about what life would be like if we were different, and it had to stop. Which meant, I wasn't going near her again. It just wasn't going to happen.

Okay, if that's what you want to tell yourself.

"You," a low voice said near my ear, "have been avoiding me."

Chills rushed down my spine as I turned my head to see Keaton standing behind me. The library was quiet and tomblike at this time of day, but I still hadn't heard him approach my table. To be fair, I hadn't really been listening—I'd thought I was safe in the very back, surrounded by the high wood shelves and out of sight from the entrance.

I'd thought wrong.

Keaton threw his big body into the chair next to me, and I was about to tell him to go away when he grabbed my chair and effortlessly dragged it around so that we were face to face. He planted his dress shoes on the outsides of my Mary Janes and his muscular thighs splayed on either side of my legs. I was trapped by his big, dumb body.

I ignored the traitorous shiver that induced in me.

"Keaton, what—"

"Listen here, Big Red," he said, leaning in and bracing his hands on the sides of my seat. I could feel the heat of his hands on my thighs through my uniform skirt. "I need this project to go well, and I can't afford to have it messed up, all right? So if you don't want to see me, that's perfectly fine. You just leave the project to me—"

"No. Way." Anger simmered in my veins as I leaned right into him. Right until I could feel his breath on my lips. "Photography is what I live for. And I am not having some rugby jock screw over the one thing I love in order to screw *me* over."

His eyebrows lifted. That one stray lock of hair he could never seem to tame brushed over his forehead as he did. "Oh, so it's all about you now? Screwing you over is all I could possibly care about?"

"What other reason could *you* have for caring about art?" I scoffed. "And *design*? Give me a break."

An expression I couldn't decipher chased itself across his face, and he broke our stare, leaning back and looking at a bookshelf while a muscle in his jaw jumped. When he met my eyes again, his gaze was cold. So very cold.

"If you care so much, then we can do this together," he said icily. "But I'm calling the shots."

"No fucking way."

"Starting now," he said, as if he hadn't heard me. "No more avoiding me. We meet every Friday night to work on this, and we meet on Saturdays too if we have to. You might be Daddy's golden girl, but the rest of us have to worry about our grades."

My jaw dropped open. The *nerve* of him—and the completely incorrect nerve! First, *Isabelle* was Daddy's golden girl, and that was a fact I could never escape, because he'd never stop reminding me of it.

Secondly, my father would never punch up my grades. Not because he cared about the ethics of it all—oh no. But because he knew how political private schools could get, and if the wrong teacher talked, his reputation would be trashed.

And thirdly: "Like *you* have to worry about GPA, Keaton Constantine, rugby captain? With your family business? With the team? Please. Your entire life is cushioned by your last name and your genetic predisposition for leg muscles. You are a walking, talking rich jock stereotype."

"And *you*," he seethed, "my uptight good-girl, are a pain in my ass. But here we are."

For a long moment, we just glared at each other, neither of us willing to surrender.

But then Keaton's eyes drifted down to my braid, which had slid over my shoulder to hang down over my chest.

His pupils dilated the tiniest amount, and then his eyes narrowed. "Why do you do that?"

"Do what?" I asked, genuinely confused by his change of mood.

"Hide your hair in that braid."

I was even more confused now. "I'm hardly hiding it. I just like it out of my face while I'm working."

"It makes it feel like a secret. Like I'm the only one who—"

With an abrupt jerk, he was off his chair and grabbing his leather satchel.

I was totally lost. "Keaton?"

He didn't look at me as he shouldered his bag. "Friday. Four o'clock in the photography lab. Be there, Iris."

And then he stalked away as fast as he had after our kiss.

We were a few weeks into the semester now, and Pembroke seemed determined to punish all its students simply for existing. I had three papers to write, half a Molière play to translate, more calc problems than I could possibly ever do, and at least three AP physics problems to do a night.

Which didn't sound like a lot, admittedly, until I started doing the physics problems and realized that each problem took an hour.

Not to mention that I was still trying to build a photography portfolio for myself, and so I was spending every spare moment outside snapping pictures and then inside the darkroom developing them. I preferred the freedom of digital, but I'd need to show in my portfolio that I could do film too, so I needed plenty of analog samples to show off.

Not for the first time, I wished I lived in a dorm, where I could study and complain and gossip with friends while I worked. Sometimes I hung out in Serafina and Sloane's room, and sometimes in Aurora's, but Sloane refused to talk when she was studying, Serafina always had random visitors dropping by, and Aurora's security person had to sit in the room while I was there since I hadn't been properly vetted by the Liechtensteiner government yet.

So home it was.

Home where my father could remind me how hard Isabelle had studied, and how easily homework came to her. Home where my mother could hide from all our family conflict like it was a spider on the wall that would eventually crawl away. Home where I could sit in my bedroom and stare out the window at the boys' dormitory across the lush, green grounds.

Where I could stare at that century-old brick building and wonder what Keaton was doing inside it.

Was he with his girlfriend? With the Hellfire Club?

Was he alone?

Was he thinking of me?

Don't be stupid, Iris.

I kept hoping Friday would never come. I hoped there would be a fire or a storm or a flood. Because I didn't know if I could face him again. I didn't know if I could survive that feeling like I wanted to scratch him and kiss him and growl insults at him while he pinned me against another bookshelf.

I'd never had a crush like this, never liked a boy like this, never felt about anybody the way I felt about Keaton. Like he had crawled under my skin. I hated him.

And . . .

I thought of him constantly.

And when the books were closed and the lights were off, I thought of our kiss. Of how good it felt to have him wedged up against me, his hands in my hair and his mouth consuming mine. Of how tight my belly had been, how I'd ached and ached between my legs as he ground himself against me.

I wanted it again, and I despised myself for my weakness. What girl was stupid enough to want a boy like *him*? A boy with a girlfriend? A boy who detested her?

Not me.

～

Friday started out with a bang—almost literally. I was sitting in my English classroom alone, about ten minutes before the bell, when a trio of beautiful girls crashed through the classroom door and strode in like leggy soldiers. They were sleek and slim, makeup perfect, their eyes full of murder.

"Are you Iris Briggs?" the one in front asked. She had dark brown hair and pale skin, muted pink lipstick and a diamond tennis bracelet. Her features were the sort of bland but forgettably pretty that came from generations of New England money.

"Um," I said. "Yes?"

The girl leaned down, bracing her hands on my desk. "Stay the *fuck* away from my boyfriend."

"Um—"

A blonde girl stepped forward too, her lips painted scarlet and a fresh hickey visible just above her shirt collar. "Don't play dumb, Briggs. McKenna told Bella who told Carlee who finally told me that she saw you kissing Keaton in the library during the first week."

Heat rushed through me—a mix of defensiveness and unease. *You didn't do anything wrong*, I reminded myself. If they were going to be angry with anyone, they should be angry with Keaton! He was the one with the girlfriend!

"You must be Clara," I said, looking back to the brunette. "Look. If you've got a problem with Keaton kissing someone else, I suggest you take it up with Keaton. He's the one who kissed me. It's not very feminist of you to scold me instead of the boy who's actually made promises to you."

Clara scowled. "I don't care about feminism right now, Briggs. I can't afford for Keaton to be seen chasing someone else. Got it?"

"It wasn't like that—"

"I don't care what it was *like*," Clara hissed. "*Don't let it happen again.* Or I will hurt you. Understood?"

"She means we'll kick your ass," the blonde supplied. I managed to dredge up her name from Serafina's lunchtime commentary a few days ago. Samantha Morgan: notorious party girl and wild child. I was very certain she was the kind of girl who would kick the shit out of me if given the chance and enough tequila.

"If you're scared or angry or whatever this is, you need to bring it to Keaton," I said as coldly as I could manage, glaring at all of them. Students began to file in for class, in pairs and trios, and I saw the moment Clara realized this was over. For now, at least.

"Keaton is mine," Clara said in a low, but clear voice as she straightened up. "And I plan to keep him at any cost—I can't afford not to, which makes me very, *very* dangerous to you. And I hope you remember that next time you're with him."

*T*he rest of the day was an anxious blur. I'd already been feeling weird and twisty about working with Keaton today, and now this Clara thing . . .

What if she found out about the project? Misunderstood the time we'd be spending together? I didn't think she and Samantha would physically hurt me—surely they had more sense than to go after the headmaster's daughter—but I also wasn't certain they *wouldn't* hurt me either. I knew Serafina would say not to worry, that she and Sloane and Aurora had my back, but still.

I didn't like it.

Photography seminar was in the lab rather than the classroom today, as we practiced with the illustration and design tools in Photoshop, which meant I didn't have to talk to Keaton or listen to him or even look at him. I kept my eyes firmly on my screen, even when I felt his gaze hot on my neck, and pretended he didn't exist.

But eventually four o'clock came, and with it, time to meet him. I strode from Aurora's room where she'd been bitching about Phineas Yates—a Hellfire boy and total manwhore—and steeled myself as I walked into the lab.

Okay. Game plan.

Lady bits, listen up.

I wasn't going to let Clara's words scare me, but I also wasn't going to kiss him or even *think* about kissing him. I was going to hold my ground, and I wasn't going to let him railroad me into something stupid for this project, because I wouldn't hear back from my safety schools until December at the earliest, and I needed my high school CV to be immaculate until then, just in case the Sorbonne fell through.

Which meant this project needed to be stunning and original enough to impress an admissions team. And that was not going to happen with a ball-playing bully like Keaton mucking it up.

You can do this.

Don't piss off Clara.

Don't take his shit.

Don't get distracted by his eyes.

Pembroke's photo lab was made of two parts: the digital lab where we worked on Photoshop today and the wet lab, or darkroom. I walked into the digital lab with its long rows of tables studded with giant, gleaming Macs and found Keaton sprawled in a chair, lazily clicking through something on one of the computers.

With some horror, I realized it was *my* computer. And he was clicking through *my* images, *my* photographs. The ones I'd scanned in earlier today to play with in Photoshop.

"You really should remember to log out of a school computer when you're done," Keaton said in a bored voice. *Click click* went his finger on the mouse. Each click felt like a gunshot in the air—echoing and final.

I'd known he would have to see my work eventually, but—but not like this. Not without my permission. Not without my preparation.

As I came closer, I could make out the individual images he was scrolling through. A picture of a leaf fading from green to gold. A shot of Isabelle in the middle of Hyde Park, looking down at her phone with a frown while the wind whipped her copper-colored hair around her face. Another one of Isabelle standing by the window in her empty London flat, her hand clenched tight around her new house key.

"Who is she?" Keaton asked.

God, of course he wanted to know about her. Everyone did. She was brilliant and beautiful and always did everything right—except picking the right boys to date. She'd always been very bad at that, for how smart and pretty she was.

I wouldn't answer. I shouldn't answer.

"My sister, Isabelle," I answered, dropping my bag on the table. Some bitterness crept into my voice. "She's single if you're interested, but she is older than us. And she's in London right now for school, so you'll have to borrow your mommy's jet to go see her."

Keaton looked at me appraisingly. "You're jealous of her."

"I'm not," I said huffily, crossing my arms.

"You are," he said. "Trust me, I know when someone is jealous of a sibling they feel like they can never live up to."

"Oh, *really*."

He shrugged, not bothered by my sarcasm and also not elaborating either. "And I wasn't asking because I thought she was hot. I was asking because she clearly means something to you. You show how lonely she is, how tense she is, and you make sure the viewer feels her loneliness too. The framing of both, the empty space around her . . . it's really well done."

My lips parted as shock poured through me. The fact that he could perceive that—perceive that I did really love Isabelle despite our differences—and he actually sounded like he knew what he was talking about left me stunned. Never in a hundred years would I have thought that Keaton Constantine could assess emotion in art.

And also . . .

"Are you complimenting me, Keaton?"

"I give compliments when they're warranted, Big Red. And these images warrant them."

It was almost patronizing. *Almost.* And I wanted to be mad about it. But when our eyes met, there was nothing but honesty and reluctant admiration in his face.

He'd meant what he said.

"Here, I want to show you something," he said, getting to his feet. He'd left his bag up by the teacher's table at the front, and he paced over to it, pulling off his blazer when he did. Which was unfortunate for me, because it meant there was now nothing disguising the firm swells of muscle under his white button-down. There was nothing hiding how his broad, hewn chest led into a flat stomach or how his waist tapered into lean and narrow hips.

Nothing hiding how tight his muscle-curved ass looked in his school trousers.

He idly loosened his tie as his other hand dug in his bag and pulled some glossy pictures free. "Tell me what you think," he said, pushing them across the table. The loosened tie made it so that I could see his throat—strong and male and oh-so-lickable.

I thought about how it would feel to have my lips against his neck. To suck the skin there until he moaned, until he growled.

Then I flushed.

"Iris?" he said. "Did you hear me?"

I gratefully took the excuse to think about something that wasn't kissing him and snagged the pictures. "Yeah. Sorry, I was just thinking about the project."

Keaton braced his palm against the back of his neck. "Yeah, so. Uh. About that." He nodded at the pictures, and I suddenly understood that he was *nervous*. The fidgeting. The hesitancy in his voice.

Keaton Constantine, god of the school, was worried about showing these to me.

And with renewed interest, I looked down.

The pictures were digital illustrations, all of them. Some incorporating photography, some freehand. And all of them were bright and vibrant and *interesting*. Even the ones that weren't perfect showed an understanding of color, of movement, that I never would have expected from a sportsball boy.

I stared down at one in particular; a drawing of a man standing with his back to the observer, his bare feet sinking into the earth, the wind tugging at his suit pants and the matching jacket draped over one arm. Even though he seemed to be standing in some kind of garden, he was looking out to where the sea glimmered in the distance, like a chilly blue invitation.

I raised my eyes to Keaton, who still stood there with his hand hanging from the nape of his neck. He was tense, unreadable. Waiting for me to say something dismissive or hurtful maybe.

I didn't. I couldn't. "This is really good, Keaton."

He relaxed the tiniest amount.

"I'm sorry I assumed you wouldn't be any good at this stuff, on account of the jockitude."

"Jockitude," he repeated, the corner of his mouth curling up ever so slightly. "What a way with words you have, headmaster's daughter."

"He's someone important to you," I decided.

His smile fell off, replaced by a careful neutrality. He started unbuttoning and rolling up his shirtsleeves—a study in forced casualness. "What makes you think he's real and not just a figment of my imagination?"

I moved some of the pictures on the table so that they were side by side. "You see this one here? Another person, but the hair is more of an idea of hair and the environment around them is static. Same here. But him? This garden? There's movement in it—the wind and the churn of the sea—and you can see how it makes him feel. And the hair isn't just *blond*; it's all different shades of gold, like he's just spent the summer outside. Like you drew him from memory."

"No," Keaton said after a minute. "Not from memory. He let me sketch him that day. It was one of the first sketches I ever made, but it took me years to finish painting it in. I couldn't bear to get it wrong."

I looked over at him.

He'd come closer as we were looking at the pictures, and I could feel the heat of him burning through my thin uniform sweater and shirt. I could see his giant shadow engulfing mine.

"Tell me about him," I whispered. It must be his father —or maybe an uncle? An older brother seemed unlikely, and the man in the picture was broad and hale and blond—so not a grandfather.

"No," he said flatly.

"Is he your father?" I pressed. "Has he seen what you made for him?"

"I'm not talking about this with you," he said, narrowing his eyes.

"You brought these pictures here for me to look at, Keaton, surely you expected me to—"

"I brought them here for the project," he said. "That's it."

"Keaton—"

I was abruptly lifted off my feet and set on the table, my feet dangling and Keaton leaning in close to my face.

"Stop asking, Iris," he said in a dangerous voice. "It's none of your business."

My entire body thrilled at having him so close. My knees kept him at a respectable distance, but his hands were braced on the edge of the table on either side of my hips, and he was close enough to kiss me.

No. Wait.

I did not want to kiss him.

I didn't need another visit from Clara.

And he was a dick the last time we kissed.

And he looked at my work without my permission.

And now he was being a *super* dick. The manhandling of me, the plucking me off my feet and setting me where he liked, as if I were nothing more than a doll for him to play with.

I tried to ignore how hot that idea was.

I tipped my chin up defiantly. "And what will you do if I don't stop asking, hmm? Tackle me like I'm on your rugby field?"

His eyes dropped back down to my braid, and he reached up to wind the soft end of it around his finger. "Tackling might be in order, Big Red."

"You wish, asshole." I made to push him away, but the moment my hands touched his hard body, my brain cut the signal short. I couldn't think about anything other than how sexy his warm muscles felt through his shirt. About how good it felt to slide my hands up from his ridged torso to his wide chest.

He gave a dark laugh. "Change your mind about something, sweetheart?"

I glared at him. "Screw you."

But I didn't pull my hands away. Instead I ran them all the way up his shoulders to his neck, to the place where his dark hair curled ever so slightly behind his ears.

His hair was almost unbelievably soft for a boy's, and thick enough to make a shampoo model jealous.

I raked my fingernails over his scalp. His eyes closed as a shiver moved through him.

I almost couldn't help what happened next; I couldn't help parting my knees. Just a little. But enough for him to notice, even with his eyes closed.

He opened his eyes and stared at the braid still clutched in his hand, and then he stared at my mouth.

"Let me kiss you," he said urgently.

Bad idea, bad idea.

"No," I said. "I'm not in the mood for your games right now."

"I'll make it worth your while," he tempted, running a finger over the top of my knee. He didn't go any farther up, just stayed there at the hem of my skirt, flirting with the edge of the fabric. I could feel every centimeter he traced as if he was branding me with his touch. Etching it, tattooing it.

"Wh-what does that mean?" I asked, my voice trembling a little. He placed his entire hand above my knee now, his thumb curling over my inner thigh, but he didn't move it. He didn't try to reach under my skirt.

"It means I'll make you come," he said in a low voice, letting go of my braid to put his free hand on my other knee. "Has anyone ever given you an orgasm, Iris? Ever made that pretty pussy happy?"

The word *pussy* from his lips was like a punch to the chest. I couldn't breathe. I felt like everything below my navel was on fire. All the reasons why this was a bad idea fled right the hell out of my mind.

"You don't even know if it's pretty," I said nonsensically.

"Oh, it would be. And it would taste even prettier."

"Taste?" I repeated faintly. I still couldn't breathe.

His firm lips were tipped up to one side in a smirk, but his eyes were deadly serious. "I know you'd taste amazing, Iris. Let me kiss your mouth, and then I'll kiss between your legs too."

The image came unbidden—Keaton's massive shoulders tucked between my thighs while his sensual mouth explored me. While that lock of hair brushed over his forehead and he used his tongue to stroke—

"We can't," I said breathlessly. "We're in the lab, anyone could see us if they were walking by—"

I was up in his arms before I even finished talking, and then we were moving back towards the darkroom door. Within seconds, we were inside, surrounded by shelves and tables and trays and sinks. Finished photographs hung from lines all around the room like paper ghosts. Some of them were mine. *Most* of them were mine.

We were bathed in red light. Keaton's normally blue eyes were a deep, royal purple. I couldn't stop staring into them.

"Iris," he rasped. His hands cradled my ass, and my thighs were wrapped around his waist and I was burning up, I was on fire. Every part of me ached for every part of him. "Let me kiss you now. Please."

My common sense was gone, my reason had fled.

There was only one answer.

"Yes," I murmured, already leaning forward. "*Yes.*"

here was a moment—a long, electric moment—when our lips touched, but we didn't move.

We stayed frozen, him holding me, my arms wrapped around his neck, his firm mouth just barely pressed against mine. It was like neither of us could believe what we were doing, like we were both paralyzed by the sudden, shocking *realness* of it. This was no longer a fantasy I played in my mind during a restless night, this was no longer a dirty reverie for extra-long showers. This was really happening, this was real life, this was Keaton Constantine gripping my body as he breathed against my lips.

And then the moment deepened, and the kiss became urgent. His lips slotted against mine, moving against them, all as his fingers plumped and squeezed my bottom, all as I panted and squirmed in his arms.

And then his tongue flickered at my lips, inviting me to open—and once I opened for him, it was all over. There was nothing but the hot stroke of his tongue against mine, nothing but our hands everywhere, everywhere, nothing but gasps and pants and groans.

He set me on a table, his mouth moving over my ear and down to my neck while his hands slid under my uniform sweater and started pulling the shirt underneath free of my waistband. Once he succeeded, he slid his hands up my bare back and then back down my spine, over and over again, like touching my skin was the only thing he wanted to do for the rest of his life.

His hands were rough and warm and big, and I wanted them everywhere on me. I wanted them against my breasts, I wanted them possessive and greedy on my waist. I wanted them in my panties, in places no one's hand but mine had ever been. I wanted him to brand me with his touch and write his name onto my skin with pleasure.

I grabbed one of his wrists and pushed his hand up to cup my breast.

"You sure, Big Red?" Keaton whispered against my mouth. "Because I want it a whole lot. It might scare you how much."

"Just—please—Keaton—"

He'd already obliged. The moment I said *please,* he'd palmed my breast, squeezing gently until I moaned. He teased my nipple through the silk of my bra cup while his other hand pulled at the bottom of my sweater.

"Get this thing off," he grunted. "I need to see you."

I was too addled with lust to disagree or to remember that my smallish breasts might not be up to scratch. Or to care that Keaton had probably seen half the school population without a shirt and that I might be found lacking. All I cared about was having more, feeling more. *More, more, more.*

Together, we peeled my sweater off and tossed it on the floor. Then both of us were fumbling with the buttons on my shirt, struggling to get them open, all while we were still trying to kiss and touch each other too.

"Fuck it," Keaton growled, and he ripped the shirt open the rest of the way, sending two buttons to lonely deaths on the darkroom floor.

I shivered as he pulled back to look at me, to look at my pink silk bra and my exposed stomach.

His eyes—still that magical, eerie purple from the red light—glowed with hunger as he took me in, but when he spoke, his voice was almost soft. Almost wondering. "You have freckles even here," he whispered.

I flushed as he traced the upper swells of my tits with his fingers, and then I moaned as he replaced his fingers with his mouth, trailing kisses all over my skin. He lowered his mouth and then sucked my hard nipple through the silk.

Jolts of heat traveled from his hot mouth straight to my pussy.

"Oh my god," I moaned. "Oh my god, oh my god." As I was losing brain cells by the second, it was all I could manage.

"I'm going to look at them now, Iris," he said, and his voice was a mix of arrogance and tenderness that I didn't think I could ever get enough of.

I nodded, but he was already working the silk cups down and freeing my breasts. The cups and underwire underneath them lifted them up and pushed them out, as if they were being presented to him, and the fact that

I still had my shirt on made it feel even dirtier somehow.

And the look on his face . . . like he'd just taken a shot of vodka. Like he'd just run across a bed of hot coals.

"Jesus fucking Christ," he muttered, his eyes raking over my freckled breasts and their straining, tight little peaks. "Jesus. Iris—I—"

He wasted no more time with words, and instead bent down to take the tip of one past his lips.

I'd never felt anything like his mouth there. *Never.* It was hot and wet and ticklish and sucking—it was *powerful*, it made me arch and whimper and twist my fingers in his hair.

"You like that?" he asked. He hadn't lifted his head, and so his words ghosted across my wet, needy flesh. "You like having your tits sucked on?"

I made a noise that was an awful lot like a whine, and he gave a dark laugh.

"Okay, sweetheart," he said. "I'll keep going."

He moved to my other breast, kissing around the pebbled skin, circling its peak, and then finally took it into his mouth, sucking and then fluttering his tongue over the stiffened tip. He scraped his teeth gently along it, and I jumped against him, and then moaned again.

"Yeah, that's it," he murmured—almost to himself. "Filthy girl."

It was then that I noticed he was idly palming his erection as he sucked on me, as if he couldn't help himself, and that thought was so hot, I couldn't stand it. The idea that I inspired lust in him, that I could make him hard, that I made him need to come . . .

"Come here, dirty thing," he said, helping me off the table. I made a noise of complaint that his mouth wasn't on my breasts anymore, and he laughed that dark laugh again, tugging on my braid and then spinning me around so that I was facing the table and he was standing right behind me.

"You'll like this, I promise," he said.

"H-how do you know? I've never done it before—*oh*—" My voice broke as Keaton's hand found the hem of my skirt and then slid up a thigh to cup me where I was covered in plain, white cotton. I wished I'd worn something sexier, something more adult, but Keaton's growl as he palmed me sounded anything but disappointed.

His fingertips pressed in a little, finding the place where my clit hid, and I shivered against him.

"You're right," he purred. "It doesn't matter if you've ever done this before, because you've never done it before with *me*. And I'm going to ruin you for any other boy who comes after."

He pushed with his fingers again, sending frissons of pleasure skating down my thighs and up my spine. "Keaton," I panted, pushing back against him. I could feel the clothed ridge of his erection against my bottom as I did, and he gave a grunt at the pressure. "Do it— please—just—just go—"

"Go where, Iris?" he whisper-asked, his fingers playing over the elastic edges of my panties now. "Inside these sweet panties? Right up against your skin?"

His actions echoed his words, and he slid his hand down the front of my panties now, his fingers toying with my silky curls, and then with the straining bundle of nerves at the apex of my thighs.

"I—please—" I didn't even know what I sounded like. Not like myself. Not like Iris Briggs who only had one goal: escape to Paris. I sounded like a girl who'd be happy to stay in this darkroom forever, and *not* to work on photography.

"Ohhh," Keaton said in mock-epiphany. "I think I know. You want me to—" His fingers went lower . . . and lower . . . "—go somewhere else, don't you?"

A lazy fingertip pushed past my folds and circled the slick secrets inside. I gasped, slamming my hands down on the table. No one had done this to me, not ever. It had only ever been my own hand, and I never could have guessed how different another person's touch would feel.

"You want me to go inside, Iris?" Keaton asked in a rough, seductive voice. "You want to feel my finger inside you?"

I nodded vigorously. "Yes, I want that. Please—*oh holy shit.*"

He'd slid a finger inside of me, giving me a moment to get used to the fullness, gently grinding his palm against my clit as he did.

"How does it feel?" he asked, a hand dropping to my hip. I realized I was grinding back against his hand, riding it and chasing the friction, and he used the hand on my hip to encourage me, guiding me until I was practically fucking his touch.

"Good." I worked the word out on a long, juddering exhale. My nipples ached in the cool air, and when I looked down, I saw my skirt bunched up near my navel and Keaton's muscled forearm disappearing into my panties.

I thought I might spontaneously combust.

"Now, my dirty little Iris can take more than one finger, can't she?"

Already a single finger felt huge. "May-maybe."

"Tell me to stop if it hurts," he said soothingly, and then he started working the second finger in. Slowly, carefully, still using his other hand on my hip to urge me against his touch, against the heel of the hand still rubbing against my clit.

And then both fingers were wedged inside me.

I heard him curse to himself when they were both inside, and then he muttered something that sounded like *tight, so fucking tight.*

And it *was* tight, it was so snug. His fingers were so much bigger than mine, longer, and even better because he knew just where to press and curl and stroke. The pressure and the pleasure became the same thing, the fullness marrying with the friction. I started riding his hand even harder, needing something, chasing something.

"*Keaton.*"

"I know, sweetheart."

"*Keaton!*"

"Let it happen," he coaxed. "Let me make you come. Right here, fucking the hand I've got shoved in your innocent panties. Come around my fingers, Iris; let me feel it."

It was his words as much as his expert touch that did me in. I came like I'd never come before, seizing and contracting and shuddering from the pleasure. Wet, sweet bliss crashed over me.

"*Oh god, oh god, oh god.*"

And that was when we heard the ripple of laughter and animated conversation coming from the direction of the digital lab. Like someone was in the hallway just outside.

Or like someone had come in and now there was only a door separating us from them.

We were about to get caught.

Keaton clapped a hand over my mouth, but he didn't stop massaging the orgasm out of me, the asshole. He just kept fingering me as I whimpered against his hand, until I was slumped against his hard body, completely spent and breathless.

And finally—*finally*—my brain started functioning again.

"Shit," I said miserably against his palm. "Oh shit."

*K*eaton eased his hand over my mouth. "Quiet, do you want to get caught?"

Meanwhile, I couldn't catch my damn breath.

What had I just done? What was I still doing? *You let Keaton Constantine fingerbang you in the darkroom.* Hell, the asshole still had his hand in my panties.

"Keaton." My voice was a whispered croak. I could not do this anymore. I had to stop.

But it feels so good.

He's the devil.

He sees you for you. Good or bad.

He's only out for himself.

No one has ever made you burn like this.

If we got caught, he would still carry on being Keaton Constantine. I would be disowned by my parents.

Silence came from outside.

We both relaxed as we realized no one was coming in to catch us.

His breath tickled the shell of my ear when he whispered. "Sorry. You okay?" He eased his fingers out of me. Gently, he smoothed my rumpled uniform skirt back down over my hips and thighs. "See? Right as rain."

I turned my head to glower at him. "Right as rain?"

He gave me a sharp nod. No harm no foul? Right as rain? In the darkroom, my solace. The place I came when I needed to get back in touch with who I was as a person.

I had let Keaton Constantine finger me. *Fingerbang me.* In the darkroom. Oh my god, I was the worst kind of teenage cliché. Hooking up with the boy I didn't like who didn't like me. A boy I could get my ass kicked for kissing. And after I'd watched my older sister Isabelle date loser after loser.

Don't be an Isabelle.

Keaton planted a kiss on my neck and my legs turned to jelly again. Damn him. I whipped around in his arms. "We have to stop this."

His dark brows furrowed as they dropped and he crossed his arms. "What?"

I licked my lips and planted my hands on the table behind me. In the red light of the darkroom his features looked more dangerous. He was all sharp angles. It made him even sexier somehow.

"You heard me. Stop. We almost got caught just now."

He rolled his eyes. "Would you relax, Briggs? Besides, if I'd gotten caught in here, no one would have said anything."

I shoved at his shoulders, but the idiot was enormous and didn't budge. "But everyone would have said something about *me*. Yeah sure, you do this kind of thing all the time. I'm the new girl. The headmaster's daughter. I can't do this. My parents will actually kill me. Not to mention, my father can think of a million ways to make both of our lives hell. I just want to have an easy year. I'm this close to freedom. Messing around with you is going to jeopardize that."

I realized my breasts were still exposed, the tips still hard and aching. His eyes dropped to them, and I felt his dick throb against me.

He licked his full bottom lip as he looked at them, and I wanted to bite it.

Jesus Christ, I was in need of a psychological evaluation. Clearly I'd inhaled too many chemicals. That's what I got for wanting to go analog for my college portfolio. I'd just switch to digital from now on. It would certainly keep my mind clearer.

"Does that matter to you, what Daddy says?" His eyes were still on my chest.

I rearranged my bra, wondering if there was such a thing as indignantly putting one's tits away. "Don't be a dick. Why can't you see that the new girl with something to prove getting caught in a compromising position with the school's golden boy isn't good for me?"

He shrugged. "Relax. A, we didn't get caught, so you can untwist your panties about that. B, no way in hell we're stopping."

I blinked up at him. Was he crazy? "What? What is wrong with you?" I started buttoning up my shirt. Well, the buttons that were left, at least. "Your rep is going to take a hit too."

I couldn't see very well, but I knew that his brow lifted. "How is this bad for me?"

"You have a girlfriend."

His brows snapped down then and he ran a hand through his blond waves. "Actually . . ."

"No. No actually. This is madness. Neither one of us can be caught in here doing this. God, what is wrong with me?" I ducked under his arm and scooped my sweater off the floor, pulling it over my head as fast as I could.

I shoved open the darkroom. Despite the earlier noises, no one was around. Keaton's pictures were still on the teacher's table, along with our bags.

He sauntered out after me. His cocky grin plastered over his face. It was a grin that said, *I just ate out the canary.* "This wasn't anything. You don't have to make such a big deal out of it."

"Okay, maybe you're used to doing things like this. Maybe you're used to cheating on your girlfriend. I am not. And truth be told, Clara could destroy me. I'm trying to get out of here with the minimum of fuss. Why can't you see that?"

A muscle in his jaw ticked as his grin slid away. "I'm not particularly thrilled about this development either. But I do know that the more I try to stay away from you, the more I seem to find myself in a scenario where I want to know what you taste like, so instead of fighting it, I'm going with the flow."

I shook my head. "Wow, such glowing affection you have for me."

"You know what this is. And let's not pretend you like me any more than I like you."

The way he said that. As if it was obvious that he wouldn't like me. That I wouldn't like him. *Do you like him?*

Maybe. No. Hell, I didn't know. He was more than the jock he portrayed. After all, wasn't I more than the overachieving goody two shoes my parents wanted me to be? He was certainly more than the spoiled rich prick he pretended to be. He put that persona on like a suit daily. The real him was probably far more complex and complicated.

After seeing his illustrations today, I had to admit to myself that maybe the good grades he had weren't a fluke. He was smarter than I'd given him credit for, and he thought things through. And he had the soul of an artist. A really gifted eye. He also was capable of working hard. Not to mention that it seemed like he had high standards like I did when it came to his art. He needed things he was putting his name on to be right.

And despite myself, I respected him. "You know I'm right."

His brow lifted. "Do you think you can stop? I'm not particularly enthused about what's happening here either. But my dick can't seem to stay away from you, so why don't we just keep going and see where it ends?"

"Where it ends is disaster. And let's not forget the one basic tenet. I don't like you."

His panty-melting grin flashed, showing a hint of dimple. "I don't like you either. But I'm stuck with you for this project. And, obviously, we can't keep our hands off each other. So stopping isn't really in the cards."

"Yes, it is. I'm done."

"Okay. Suit yourself. But you'll be back." He stepped close, and automatically, I licked my lips, readying them for his kisses. "I'm irresistible. No one can stay away for long."

I was the problem. I had to build better walls and protect myself from whatever attacks he had against my defenses. I could do this. I stepped back. "No. Take that smile to your girlfriend. I'm out."

He stopped immediately in his tracks and held up his hands. "Okay, you say no, I stop. But I will say this. Your nipples are still hard for me. I know exactly how they feel, how they taste. They like me. You don't even have to. Not all of you has to like me, you know? But you come to me next time."

"I am not coming to you. You are the most pompous, arrogant, egotistical—"

"You realize all those mean the same thing, right?"

I wanted to hit him. I've never been violent a day in my life. I had a vicious tongue when pushed, but violent, no.

But right now, I could have kicked him in the shins and have been perfectly happy to do so.

He didn't take another step towards me. But he did lean on the table between us, planting his hands, and I could see the thick veins running through his very stellar forearms. *Jesus Christ.* "I won't touch you if you don't want me to. The question is, don't you want me to?"

"No, because we are being reckless. And you don't like me either. You can get ass anywhere in this school. Like from your girlfriend."

There was that frown again. "Don't you worry about Clara. Worry about yourself."

"I'm sorry, but I'm not a violent person. Clara seems like she is. She threatened to kick my ass. I don't even have a posse to back me up."

"What do you call Serafina and Sloane?"

"They're very nice. I call them friends. And friends don't ask friends to kick somebody else's ass on their behalf."

He shrugged. "Guys do it all the time."

I fussed with my braid, rearranging it over one shoulder. Keaton scowled at it. "Look, let's just chalk today up to an accident."

The corner of his lips tipped into a smirk. "An accident? One where I asked you if I could kiss you, and you said yes. And then you kissed me back. Then our hands were all over each other. And I was pulling down your bra and sucking on your tits. Then I turned you around against that table in there and slid my hands into your panties. You're calling that an accident?"

If my panties hadn't already been soaked, that would have done the trick. Every muscle in my pelvic region relaxed, and then clenched, starting this pulsing motion that I couldn't stop. I wanted him.

"Look, that wasn't supposed to happen, is what I meant to say. And it won't happen again because you and me, we're just too unalike. We don't like each other; we don't even know each other."

"You want to know me? Why does it have to be like that? Why can't it just be that we like hooking up?"

"That's not who I am. I need to actually like the person that I make out with. I get it. You're a guy. You don't have to like anyone. Hell, I don't think you've liked anyone in your day-to-day life. But I need that."

A frown furrowed his brow. "You really don't like me?"

I swallowed and then lied. "Nope. You're a half-decent artist, but too rash. Too smug for your own good. Cocky. Used to being good at everything, and you think you own this place. You don't."

"Well, tell me how you really feel."

I leaned on the table. I'd opted for the same casual attitude that he had. "I can't do this. I already have all these stupid expectations. And I can feel myself in a pressure cooker. I don't need you fucking with my head too. So just back off. I'm not going to say yes anymore."

He lifted a brow then and brought his fingers to his lips and sucked.

Panties down. Panties down. They were on fire. He was licking my taste off them.

He closed his eyes and moaned, licking them clean before pulling them free. "Well, if I'm not going to have another taste, might as well enjoy the one I just had."

My mouth hung open as I watched him march out of the lab. Keaton Constantine was an asshole.

Keaton Constantine was also the sexiest guy I had ever seen in my life.

And I was a liar. I liked him. I just didn't want to.

What the fuck was I going to do?

"**W**hy the fuck are you so tense, man?" Phin asked, bumping against my shoulder. "Fucking *relax*."

"I'm plenty relaxed," I growled. *Way to be relaxed, Constantine.*

"No, you're not," Lennox drawled in his British accent. "You look like you're ready for bloody murder."

I took a drink of my lukewarm beer and made a face. I should have brought some of the good stuff from my room. Or better yet, I should have made Rhys or Lennox load me up with the high-caliber booze they always seemed to have on hand.

Bonfire party beer was *awful*.

The taste of victory, however, was very sweet, and I tried to savor it as I watched the Croft Wells bastards scowl and toss back shots of Everclear on their side of the fire. We'd handed their asses to them in the exhibition game this afternoon, and even though this aftergame party deep in the woods was supposed to be all about drinking and screwing and lighting shit on fire, there was still plenty of bad blood in the air.

Not that I minded. It felt good to win.

Then why is Phin right? Why can't you relax?

"Is Clara doing okay?" Owen asked. I couldn't tell if he was genuinely interested or if he wanted to move the conversation past an awkward moment—or if he was just bored. With Owen, it really could be all three things at once. Even though we were all rich motherfuckers, he was the most stereotypical rich motherfucker of us all, like he was trapped in an Edith Wharton novel or something.

Snooty, but also unfailingly mannered while he was judging your ass.

It was unsettling at times, like right now, when I couldn't tell if he was simply being nice or not.

"Clara's fine, she just needed to rest," I said, taking another drink to cover the half-lie. We'd made the obligatory appearance early on—her clinging to my arm and loudly praising my skill on the field—and then she'd claimed a headache and went back to the dorms, where no doubt she'd be underneath her *actual* boyfriend for the rest of the night.

As usual, our act seemed to fool everyone, but it would only keep fooling everyone if I didn't do something stupid.

Something stupid like kissing Iris in public again, for example.

Clara's your friend. You're keeping her parents off her back.

And you're keeping your parent off yours too, Constantine.

Keep playing the game.

Trouble was, the game seemed a whole hell of a lot longer now that Iris was in the mix. Something about that copper hair and those sweet blue eyes. That gorgeous mouth, which could never seem to stop sassing off to me—except when I kissed it quiet of course. Something about those fucking *freckles*.

And her taste.

I'd been jerking off to the memory of that taste for over a week. I'd even caught myself licking my lips, as if I thought it might still be lingering there.

I had to have it again.

"You're looking for her," a cold voice said. I slid my gaze over to Rhys, who was staring back at me with something almost like malice. "The new girl."

"I'm not," I replied automatically, even though I knew I had been. "I don't care if she comes."

Even though I told her about the bonfire yesterday. Even though I told her she should come.

We'd been working on the project out on the back lawn —her request, probably to avoid being in the same spots where we'd fooled around—and she'd been so buttoned up again, so remote. Quiet like she'd been the first day of school, with hardly a word to say to me that wasn't about possible landscapes or integrating illustration.

Like I didn't know about the freckles on her tits.

Like I didn't know how she tasted between her thighs.

I'd known what she was doing, and it pissed me off. She knew when we argued, we ended up kissing. She also knew that when we didn't argue—when we actually shared shit and talked—we also ended up kissing.

So she was keeping all that fire and all that sweetness locked up, far away from me and my kisses.

I'd hated it. I still hated it.

So I'd invited her tonight, hoping like a jackass that she'd also come to my game and see me play. How childish was that?

"I'm not looking for her," I repeated, after Rhys wouldn't stop staring at me. "I swear."

"Hmm."

On the other side of the fire, Samantha Morgan had waltzed over to the Croft Wells kids, bringing the gift of a beer bong and a short skirt. The losers perked up immediately, smiling and posturing and jockeying for a position next to her.

"Samantha's going to be okay, right?" I asked.

"Emma and Romola are with her," Rhys observed. "And you know Owen won't let anything untoward happen. Not on his prissy watch."

"Making sure assholes don't do anything shitty isn't exactly prissy."

"It will feel a lot prissier after he gets on your case for making out with the new girl tonight."

"I told you, I don't care if she comes or not."

Rhys looked away. His sharp mouth was curved in a frown. "Good. Because if she comes, she'll draw attention."

Anger surged through me as I realized he was right. All the Croft Wells boys currently salivating over Samantha would shred each other bloody for a chance with Iris, with her pretty eyes and her even prettier mouth. Every part of her practically screamed delicious innocence, and there's nothing that dirty assholes loved more than innocence. I should know.

Rhys noticed my scowl at the group on the other side of the fire, and then sighed. "I didn't mean them, dumbass. I meant her *father*. The last thing you want is Headmaster Briggs associating rugby with whatever—" he gestured at Samantha, who was currently riding a Croft kid's back like a horse and doing a shot at the same time "—this is."

Fuck. He was right. Briggs had one goal, and one goal only—turn Pembroke into a fully-fledged Ivy mill. It was pretty close already; save for the kids who took eternal gap years and the ones who turned into social media influencers, most of us ended up at an Ivy or the international equivalent. But most wasn't good enough for Briggs. Most wouldn't bring in those sweet alumni dollars.

And the hard truth was as much as alumni loved the pride and the legacy of things like rugby and lacrosse and rowing, they didn't bring the wow factor the way those college acceptance stats did.

Rhys was right. We were already in Briggs' crosshairs. The last thing I needed was for him to catch Iris at a party that was practically sponsored by Gentleman Jack and Plan B.

Except then Iris appeared between the trees, and I forgot everything I needed.

Other than her.

I stepped forward, and Rhys caught my elbow. "Bad fucking idea, Constantine."

I shook him off. "I'm not going to do anything stupid."

"Define *stupid*," Rhys muttered, but he didn't try to stop me as I crossed the clearing to meet Iris.

The night was the first real night of the New England autumn—with a faint chill in the air and a restless breeze moving through the just-turning leaves above us. Which meant that Iris had bright pink cheeks as she stepped into the firelight. I wondered if her nipples were hard from the cold too.

I wondered if she'd let me warm them up for her.

She was wearing a good-girl outfit tonight—the kind of outfit that made a boy like me want to filthy her up. Thick black tights and a cute dress that looked like a sweater—long enough to be demure, but still short enough for me to easily reach under it if I wanted. Which I did.

She also had her bright hair in two braids again, and my hands flexed as I thought about taking them apart and sifting my fingers through her tresses. Rubbing my mouth against them.

God, she made me crazy. There were so many hot girls here—so many hot girls in the town not two miles away —and yet *this* girl was the one I couldn't get enough of. This tiny, mouthy, hyper-disciplined waif of a girl.

Before I could grab her and haul her off into the darkness, Serafina, Sloane, and Aurora appeared behind her, their happy expressions melting into ferocious battle faces as they saw me.

"No," Serafina said, striding past Iris to get straight to me. She put her finger against my chest. "You don't get to bother her tonight."

I held up my hands. "No bothering. I just want to talk about our project."

"*Un.* Likely," Aurora pronounced. "You've got that bothering look in your eye."

"Guys, it's okay," Iris said, stepping closer to me and pushing Serafina's finger down. "I promise. Keaton is going to be the perfect gentleman. Isn't that right, Keaton?"

There was nothing gentlemanly about my thoughts right then, or the semi that was stiffening behind my fly, but I nodded. "As gentlemanly as Owen."

Everyone except Iris groaned. Owen's brooding addiction to manners was known to more than just us in the Hellfire Club. He wouldn't be caught dead bothering a girl—he allowed girls to bother *him* and then made them tidy up before they left.

"Fine," Serafina said. "Channel Owen. And if I find out you put one cleat out of line, I'm going to let Sloane murder you."

I looked over to Sloane who was wearing a black leather jacket and the kind of boots you might wear to bury a body in.

"Deal," I said, and then I grabbed Iris's hand and tugged her away.

I led her away from the fire and into the trees, where clusters of students lazed on Nantucket Looms blankets. There was the sound of lighters lighting up weed, the sounds of kissing and giggling, until it all faded away, and it was just me and Iris alone in the woods, with only the faint orange glow of the fire in the distance to show us where we came from. Iris yanked her hand out of mine as soon as we cleared the last of the sex-and-drugs blankets.

"Follow me into the woods said the Big Bad Wolf to Red Riding Hood," Iris said.

"Shh," I said, turning onto a little path between the trees. "You can almost hear it."

"Hear what—oh! It's a river!"

Iris ran down to the edge of the water excitedly.

River was being generous—it was a brook at best, narrow and splashy and shallow. But even I had to admit it was pretty, and even better, this part of it was surrounded by flat rocks and soft grass. Perfect for more Iris kisses.

I sat down on the grassy bank and then reached up for her. "Come here."

She narrowed her eyes at me, choosing to sit far enough away that I couldn't reach her without lunging. "We're not making out again, Keaton."

"Okay," I said. "We can skip the kissing if you like. I don't mind getting straight to the part where I make you come."

The nearly full moon was bright enough that I could see her cheeks darken. "We said we weren't going to do that again."

"No, you said that." I lifted an eyebrow at her. "I don't recall agreeing to anything."

"You agreed that we didn't like each other."

"And then I said that it has nothing to do with this," I pointed out, moving my hand between us. "I can make your pussy feel good, and then you can get right back to hating me."

"Wow. The moonlight makes you so romantic," she said in a dry tone, turning back to look at the brook.

I was ready with a quip, I really was, but there was something about the way she looked right then, drawing her knees up to her chest and staring down at the water, that made the sarcastic words disappear.

She didn't look sad, necessarily, but she looked—I didn't know—*lonely* maybe. Or alone in her own thoughts.

I didn't like the idea of her feeling lonely. I didn't know why, because I obviously didn't give a damn how she felt unless it ended with my mouth on her tits. But somehow, I found myself moving closer to her anyway. I found myself sliding an arm around her shoulders—not to yank her into my lap like I'd wanted to earlier—but simply to hold her close. To make sure she was warm. To make sure she knew she wasn't actually alone.

I was probably a shit boyfriend, a shit friend, and a shit guy in general, but I could do this one thing. I could make someone feel like they weren't the only person on the planet.

"You're ruminative tonight, Big Red."

"*Ruminative* is an awfully big word for a boy who can run as fast as you."

Pleasure curled through my chest.

"Does that mean you've watched me run, Iris? Did you come to the game today?"

She ducked her head down, smiling a little at her knees. "Maybe."

"Maybe?" I reached over and lifted her chin. "You watched me play?"

Another flush under those freckles. "Okay, yes. I watched. You have very nice legs."

I laughed. "Is that all you took away from it, sweetheart? That rugby players wear shorts?"

"Well, and that you apparently have no fear." She shook her head in disbelief. "I really thought you were going to leave that field on a stretcher."

I shrugged like it was no big deal. Actually, I'd had to pop some Advil for a nasty bruise on my shoulder and there was a grassy scrape along one thigh that had stung like hell in the shower after the game, but my pride refused to tell her all that.

"Guess I'm just tough," I said casually.

"Uh-huh," she said, like she wasn't buying it. And she probably wasn't. She'd been able to see past my bullshit since the moment she stepped on campus.

"You didn't respond to my observation," I reminded her. "Why so pensive? Most girls would already be in my lap by now."

It was the wrong thing to say, and it earned me a fierce scowl. "Maybe I'm the only girl who happens to care that you're dating Clara."

God. This Clara thing. It was going to kill me, it really was—or at least my neglected erection. I wanted to tell Iris the truth—that Clara and I only pretended to date to keep our parents happy. That she needed the cover for dating the boy she really loved, who was too poor and too anonymous to ever win her parents' approval.

That we were riding the lie until graduation, when we'd be free. Or at least freer than before.

I opened my mouth to say it all, and then I hesitated, remembering Rhys's words from earlier. As much as I wanted this girl, as much as she dominated my thoughts, I couldn't forget who her father was. I couldn't forget that I barely knew her.

Clara had begged me to keep our real relationship terms a secret, and I'd honored that shit. Even the Hell-fire Club didn't know our relationship was fake. I didn't know if Iris was the kind of girl who could keep a secret or not, and if she couldn't—if she told Serafina or Aurora—then there was no telling how many other people would hear about it. And then I would've broken my oldest friend's trust *and* screwed us both over with our parents.

Fuck.

"It's complicated with Clara," I finally said. "It's not like I can't do this, though. With you."

She frowned at me. "That's not how Clara made it sound."

Dammit, Clara. "She's worried about appearances, that's all. No one can see us here. It can be our little secret."

Iris turned back to the water, a thick red braid moving over her shoulder. "I don't want to be a secret. I'm already an embarrassment to my parents."

I scoffed. "That can't possibly be true."

She glared at me. "Want to bet?"

"You get amazing grades, you never get in trouble, you're like straight from the Good Girl Factory. There's no way they're embarrassed."

"They want me to be my older sister. They want me to go to Harvard or Brown or Dartmouth. They want me to study law. They want me to make *them* look better."

"And you don't want Harvard? You don't want to be a lawyer?"

She blew out a long breath. "I want to do what I love, and I want to do it far away from here. I want to spend hours waiting for the perfect shot of fog rolling over the Seine. I want to go into the catacombs and picnic in the Tuileries and people-watch from a cafe while I'm eating delicious pastries. I want to fall in love with a French guy and walk through the city hand in hand and go to operas and ballets. I want to start my real life and start being who I really am."

Fall in love with a French guy?

A wave of irritated possessiveness rolled through me, just at the thought of some hypothetical moron holding her hand and doing all that romantic crap with her.

She took a deep breath, looking surprised at herself. "Sorry," she mumbled. "I don't normally go off like that."

"I don't mind," I told her. *Everything but the part about the French guy, at least.*

"It's silly."

"It's not silly. But you *are* wrong about something."

Her eyebrow arched a little in defiance. "Oh really. I'm wrong about something? Care to mansplain myself to me?"

"I like it when you're saucy," I said, and I finally did what I'd wanted to do for the past ten minutes, and I scooped her into my lap.

This time, she let me.

"You're not wrong about yourself, Iris, but you are wrong that there's such a thing as *real life*. This, right now, is real life, and you have the power to make it the way you want. Are you always going to be what everyone else wants you to be?"

She tucked her head against my chest as I finished.

"Or are you going to do what might actually make you happy?" I asked her, more gently than I thought I was capable of—maybe it was because I was also asking myself at the same time.

Am I going to keep trying to please everyone else?

Even if it keeps me away from what I really want?

She tilted her head to look up at me. "And what do you think would make me happy, Keaton?" she asked. Her voice was soft, a little husky. Her pupils were huge pools of obsidian ringed in cobalt.

Fuck. I needed this. I needed *her*.

"I can make you happy," I growled, tugging the hair ties off those terrible, wonderful braids. Terrible because they kept all that pretty, Titian hair locked away from me. Wonderful because they gave me moments like this, the moments when I got to free it and feel it tumbling cool and silky over my fingers. It was like the first pour from a good bottle of scotch. It was like the first firm stroke of my hand when I needed to get off. It was the promise of something decadent, with so much more decadence to come.

"Can you?" she whispered, sliding her hands up my chest. Through the thin fabric of my long-sleeved Baracuta tee, I could feel the warmth of her hands as they moved over my pectoral muscles to my collarbone and then to my neck. She stroked her fingers over a spot behind my ear, and I nearly had a heart attack.

I wanted her to do it forever.

I wanted to flip her over onto her back and nibble on her fingers until she begged me to make her come.

"I can make you very happy," I informed her in a growl, moving her so that she properly straddled my lap and then working my hands into that mass of glorious hair.

"You shouldn't," she said, still whispering. "*We* shouldn't do this."

"We're not doing anything."

"You're going to—" Her voice went shy and husky all at once. "You're going to stick your hand in my panties and make me come again."

"I promise not to make you come with my hands." I said absolutely nothing about my tongue.

"We still shouldn't—"

"Clara doesn't have anything to do with us."

"*Us* has to do with us. We don't even like each other!"

My hands were still in her hair. "I like you plenty right now, Iris Briggs. Let me kiss you."

Her lips parted, and I could see the hesitation and need warring on her face. She wanted it.

She just didn't *want* to want it.

But then she shifted a little in my lap, lining up the hard ridge of my need against her center, and a heavy shudder moved through her body as she moved away again. "Just a kiss," she murmured, drugged by the friction she'd felt between our lower halves. "Just one. Or two."

I needed no other encouragement. I pulled her closer and took her mouth with my own.

It was everything I remembered.

It was as hot and sweet and wild; it was vicious and delicious. She tasted clean and sweet, like strawberries, and her lips were so soft, the kind of soft that wet dreams were made of. When she let my tongue past her lips to stroke against hers, heat surged down to my groin. I was so close to losing it and we hadn't even *done* anything yet.

We'd kissed.

We'd *kissed*, and now I was trying not to come.

What was this girl doing to me?

There was too much of her I needed to touch—I needed her mouth and I needed the soft hollow of her neck and I needed my hands in her hair and I also needed them shaped to the curves of her tits.

I needed them on her hips, pressing her harder against me, and I needed them up her dress, where I could make her moan and whimper for me again.

"Keaton," she murmured, dipping her face to suck at my neck. I tilted my head, offering more skin for her mouth, as I slid my hands down to her hips and guided her firmly against my lap. Now, with her dress pushed up and her legs wrapped around me, the soft warmth between her legs was once again pressed directly against my denim-covered erection.

"Oh my god," she whispered, rocking against it and shivering. "Oh my god. We shouldn't . . ."

"Just for a while longer," I said in between searing kisses. "Just a few more moments."

She nodded her head, a small noise whimpering in the back of her throat as she screwed her hips against mine. "We'll stop. Very soon."

"That's right," I told her. "As soon as you want. *Fuck*, Iris, that feels so good."

I moved my hands from her hips to her ass and helped her. Helped her grind down on me, watching her face as she did. Copper hair tumbled everywhere, and the moonlight caught along the tips of her long eyelashes. I seriously never thought about shit in this way, but she looked like a princess. Like a princess about to come from riding my lap.

"Feel good, baby?" I rasped, working her harder over me. My cock *ached* like a motherfucker, and my thighs were tight from trying to hold back the orgasm that wanted to hit like a tsunami. But I wouldn't come until she did. No matter how good it felt to have her soft pussy grinding over me. No matter how sexy it was to feel her thighs around my hips.

No matter how fuckable she looked right now, with her lips parted and her eyes wide.

"Keaton," she whispered, and then shuddered over me, rocking and rocking, her head dropping down to roll on my shoulder.

I held her tight, loving every fucking minute of it: her shivers and her pants, how eagerly she kept rubbing herself against me, as if she was chasing every last second of her orgasm.

The only thing I wished was that I could feel it for myself—that I had my fingers inside her, or my dick—

Shit.

Even just thinking about being inside had my cock leaking precum inside my boxers. While she was still coming down from her release, I rolled us back and over—fast enough to make her gasp, but careful enough to make sure she was comfortable—so that she was on her back and I was over her.

"I want to see you," I said desperately, getting to my knees and pushing her dress back up to her hips. "I want to see where you came for me."

Her eyelashes fluttered—gleaming silver from the moonlight—and a slow, lazy smile curved her lips. She was all satiation now, all loose limbs and dozy eyes, while I was strung as tight as a piano wire.

"Okay, Keaton," she said, all the pleasure I'd just given her still thick in her voice. She parted her thighs even more in invitation. "You can look."

I was already moving my hands up her thighs, sliding my palms over the synthetic material of her tights. They were thick as far as tights went, but as worked up as I was, they were no match for me. I tore a hole right between her legs, ripping it open enough to get a good look at the pink cotton panties underneath.

I hooked them to the side, and for the first time, I got to see her. I got to see where she was wet and soft, just for me.

"Babe." My voice was rough.

She grabbed my shirt and pulled me down to kiss her again, her hips undulating lazily underneath me.

"You want more?" I whispered against her lips. "You want me to give you another one?"

She nodded, still kissing me, and then sighing as I moved a thigh between her legs for her to move against. By this point, my dick could have hammered nails, and I had to bite my lip to keep from grunting every time she accidentally brushed against it. I'd never gone so long without getting off, and I couldn't even say why exactly, other than that I would tear off my own arm before I stopped right now. I had to make her feel good again.

"What about you?" she asked between kisses. Her hand slid down, down, and then her fingers skated over me. Showers of sparks chased her touch—down my belly, deep in my groin, all along the aching length.

I covered her hand with mine. "You want to make this feel better?" I breathed. "I can show you how."

Her heavenly blue eyes were wide on mine as I guided her into rubbing me, as I decided I needed to pop open the button of my fly—

Honk.

Honk honk.

Hooooonk.

"Shit."

Her face screwed up in confusion. "Are those cars?"

Honk honk honk.

"Yeah. Shit. Here, let me help you up—" I rolled to my feet and took her hands, hauling her easily to standing and then tugging her dress down. Her hair was tousled and her lips were swollen and her tights were torn—but the tights were hidden by her dress and the rest could be chalked up to drinking.

And not, you know, having her pussy seen to by the rugby captain.

"The honks mean we're being busted," I said, taking her hand and tugging her away from the river and towards the bonfire. "We need to get back to the school."

"Okay," she said, looking pale and worried, and I stopped.

"You've never been to a party getting busted before?"

She shook her head.

"You'll be fine," I reassured her. "You haven't been drinking and we don't have any alcohol on us. If someone stops us, the worst that will happen is they tell us to go home."

"If you say so," she muttered as we started walking again, but she didn't sound convinced. All around us were scrambling students, some of them dumping out liquor or weed, others trying to cram it in their pockets and then make a run for it through the trees, taking the long way back to the school.

Me, I preferred the direct route. I figured if it were the cops or school admin, either way, they'd already have their hands full with Samantha Morgan and the Croft Wells kids. We'd just waltz past all the mess and then right back onto the school grounds.

Except there was one thing I wasn't counting on when I reached the bonfire clearing.

One *person*.

I dropped Iris's hand.

"Daddy," she whispered. It could have been horror, or it could have been relief, I didn't know her well enough to say.

You don't know her at all.

"Did you tell him about the party?" I asked, looking over at her. Headmaster Briggs was striding towards us, thunder in his face, and all I could think was that Rhys was right.

She'll draw attention.

The last thing you want is Headmaster Briggs associating rugby with whatever this is.

Shit. Had I just fucked over the entire team—and myself—by fucking around with the headmaster's daughter?

Iris's face was difficult to read. She seemed hurt or indignant or both. "Of course I didn't," she hissed. "Do you think I would have . . . *you know* . . . if I knew he was coming?"

"I don't know, Big Red. How badly would you like to see me in trouble?"

Her mouth gaped. "*What?*"

"Were you bait?"

She closed her mouth then, and her eyes narrowed. "I hate you."

"So you say. And so here we are." I nodded at Head-master Briggs, who'd finally reached us, his cheeks florid with rage.

I knew I should have run then. And I could have; in the dim, flickering light, he probably hadn't gotten a good look at my face and would have thought me just another fleeing teenager. But as suspicious of Iris as I was, as pissed as I was about what this might mean for the team, I couldn't leave her there. I didn't know why.

Something about her made me stupid as hell, I guess.

I drew myself up to my full height, fully expecting the headmaster to start laying into me.

Instead, it was as if he didn't even see me at all. He only had furious eyes for his daughter. "You," he said coldly to her. "Home with me. *Now*."

She didn't look at me. But she didn't have to look at me for me to sense that something normally bright and vibrant inside of her had gone dim. And it was her father's fault.

She stepped forward, and they both turned and walked away, leaving me in no trouble at all.

And yet still feeling guiltier than ever.

*T*here was a very specific format to a Milo Briggs lecture.

It was always guaran-goddamn-teed to start with stern disappointment sewn in with some mild derision.

Add a little dash of expectation, some confusion as to how you could have possibly disappointed when you were a Briggs, and then, finally, some love.

There was always love intertwined, which should have made it hurt less, but somehow always managed to make it worse. Because at the end of the day no matter what, I knew my parents wanted the best for me.

The problem was they never actually listened to me or asked me what *I* wanted. They just had their plans laid out, *their* expectations. And I was expected to comply.

To follow along, to do as I was told. To follow the rules. And all I wanted to do was to break the rules.

Total lie.

I didn't want to break the rules. That was ridiculous. Who *wanted* to break rules? I liked rules. Rules guided things. I just liked the rules that made sense. If a rule seemed dumb to me or arbitrary, then I was less inclined to follow it. The number one important thing to me was my freedom. I just wanted to be out of here. And it was almost within my reach. Unfortunately, my father had other plans for me.

"I cannot believe you, Iris. Out cavorting with god knows who, drinking and doing god knows what."

He had a point about the god knows what part. I knew that this was the portion of the lecture where I was supposed to inject the, "I'm sorry, Daddy."

Instead I said, "What is it you can't believe?"

I blinked. Then blinked again. Wondering if somehow I'd become a ventriloquist dummy. That was not what I intended to say.

His brows furrowed. Likely because I had never ever said anything like that to him before. "Iris, I know a move to a new school in your senior year was not . . . ideal."

"Not ideal?" He was kidding right? He'd gotten the new post right after Isabelle had gone to school in London. "You uprooted my whole high-school experience. You didn't even ask. And when I asked if I could stay with Aunt Helen, you said no. 'A family has to stay together,' you said."

He sighed. Clearly flummoxed as to where this newfound mouthiness was coming from. The truth was I was always mouthy. Just, I didn't usually say things out loud. But for some reason, the comebacks, the sly comments, the quick wit, they all came out when I was talking to Keaton. It was easy to forget to control myself with him. Usually because he was making me so mad.

Also for other *reasons.*

But for my parents, I bit my tongue. I knew how important it was to present the right image. But it was like being with Keaton had loosened something in me, and that half of a fuck I had left had dwindled to nearly nothing. Now, it was open season and I couldn't stop the words from tripping and dancing and twirling out of my mouth.

"Iris Briggs. I am your father. I mean, to find you at a party? I am disappointed. Fine, you're young. I know you need to have some social experiences. But you, with those kids from Croft Wells? From the Hellfire Club? What in the world is wrong with you?"

"Aren't you always the one that says, 'Make new friends, get to know the school culture. Immerse yourself fully.'" I tapped my chin. "That was you, right? Or should I go round up Mom and see if she remembers who said those words? It was either her or you. Or hey, maybe it was Isabelle. But ah wait, that's right. Isabelle is not here to check with you, because you let my sister go off to London."

"She's off to study economics."

That was the crux of it. Unlike my sister, I was being impractical. They didn't want me studying photography. And that chafed me raw.

"Look, Iris. Your mother and I, we love you."

"And I love you. I just, I feel trapped, Daddy."

"And that is not what we want for you. It's your senior year and we didn't want to just leave you behind with your aunt. We are a family."

That seed of discontentment that had planted itself in my belly, rooted, and had started to sprout little leaves, blossomed into a blood-red flower, covered in thorns. I knew they loved me. And I loved them. I just didn't want what they wanted for me. And they were unwilling to listen.

"Daddy, I don't understand what the problem is. I have straight As. I work hard, I've been making friends. Getting to know people."

"But you're distracted. I can tell. Back-to-school night, where were you? Your mother and I were counting on you. You know the rule. You know your role. Whatever the new school is, you make everyone feel welcome and that you are excited to be a student there. We did not have that this time."

I muttered under my breath, "I'm sorry, a student needed me."

"What student? Was something wrong?"

I swallowed down the pang of jealousy at his immediate concern for some fictitious student. My jealousy was only salved by the knowledge that the student was Keaton Constantine. And my father would not be too worried about him.

"I took care of it. But that's what I was doing. So sorry I couldn't be by your side."

He shook his head. "Iris, we need you to get things together. Honestly, your mother said it's like you're not even interested in the college application process."

More like I wasn't interested in the applications they wanted me to be interested in. "Oh that. I filled out some of the forms you gave me." I had done my essays. Or rather, I'd taken a series of essays through school and from working on past school newspapers as well as my blog and repurposed several of them to fit the questions being asked. "What about my applications?"

"What about them is you don't seem interested. Is there anywhere that you're dying to go? We could make calls. You're not campaigning for yourself, Iris."

"I've applied to my dream school and several safeties," I hedged, hoping he wouldn't ask for more details. "Well, I'll see where I get in and then I'll make a decision."

He softened then. We were about to get to the I-love-you portion of the lecture. "I need you to buckle down and show me you want this."

I did want this. I wanted my parents' approval. Just not at the expense of myself.

"Iris, we need you to get back to your focus. You have opportunities awaiting you. Can you show me that you care? Can you show me that you're not distracted? That you're not going to let some boys and wild parties get the better of your senior year? Screwing around is not what you do."

My brow furrowed. "Daddy, I went to *one* party. I didn't even drink. I hung out with kids from the school. I didn't even talk to the kids from the other school. I did everything that I was supposed to do and then some. But the first time I go to a party, you're mad?"

"I'm not mad. I'm disappointed. If you'd just told us. . ."

"Oh my god, so I'm that kid. The one who narcs on her friends. Besides, what is so wrong with a party?"

"You forget I was young once."

"Oh no. I don't forget. You keep telling me. But you keep acting seriously uncool."

He sat back, crossed his arms. "All right, fine, you can go to your room now. But finish the rest of your applications, would you?"

I couldn't give a shit about Harvard—where he wanted me to go. Columbia didn't interest me, although NYU did, and I'd applied there as a safety. My mother's alma mater of Brown held zero appeal. But of course, she had already made all the calls to the director of admissions and the alumni board. Dad had gone to Dartmouth. And so that's where he was campaigning for.

Neither one of them wanted Yale.

God forbid.

So Harvard was the compromise. *Obvi.*

I shook my head. Neither one of them had asked me where *I* wanted to go. What dream would make me fly, soar. The good news was I was eighteen. My college fund was fully funded. And I could get a loan for living expenses. I had it all figured out. And they couldn't stop me.

With my father's disappointed eyes watching me warily, I stood and grabbed my backpack off the floor. "If we're done, Daddy?"

"Yeah, we're done. Just try to stay out of trouble, Iris. I've never had to say that to you before, but maybe without your sister here as an example, you need to hear it. But I really don't want that to be our relationship now."

I refrained from rolling my eyes for fear that one of them would get so far lodged I wouldn't be able to get it back. Izzy, perfect Izzy, brilliant and scarlet-haired and beautiful. A hard act to follow.

There was a small part of me that wanted to be like her. I wished I could just toe the line. But I didn't want to. I wanted to be in Paris. I wanted to have freedom.

Problem was Dad wasn't wrong about me being distracted. Keaton Constantine had me twisted. God, I'd been making out with him, at a party. Lying down. He'd been grinding on me with his hand up my dress and that delicious pressure right at the juncture of my thighs.

I had been flying. Feeling like my skin was on fire and I was vibrating all at once. It felt so good. But god, he was so evil. Swear to god if he somehow still managed to tank this project for me, I was going to kill him. Not to mention that fucking *bait* comment!

I was super going to kill him.

Funny how my usual Keaton Constantine feelings included thoughts of murder. I thought about it frequently. I wondered if I could hit him hard enough to make him pass out, if I could throttle him. I wondered what would happen if I took my dad's car and just ran him over.

And then on the other hand, I wondered how far this thing between us—the whispered hushed secrets and soul baring—was going to go. And, of course, there was the desperate forbidden deliciousness, the need to be near him even when I knew I hated him.

You don't hate him.

I shoved that thought aside. What the fuck? I absolutely *did* hate him. I hated everything about him. The kind of guy he was, that smug alpha asshole. I hated alpha guys. Loathed them. I didn't necessarily want a beta guy either. But I hated that cocksure I-know-everything-and-you-know-nothing kind of attitude. It made me want to punch things.

That attitude roiled against my need for independence, and so I stayed away from guys like that. But somehow, I couldn't stay away from Keaton. It didn't matter how much I hated him.

You don't hate him.

God, I did. *Please, God, let me still hate him.*

The problem was I knew that was right. I didn't hate him.

Being lectured now, that sucked. And the first person I wanted to talk to was him. Not to Sera, not Sloane. Not even Rachel from back home. I wanted Keaton.

From a few of the things he'd said about his parents, I got the impression he would understand. That he would feel me and my annoyance so hard. And the disappointment, and the need to be my own person. The need to break free. I knew he would get it.

Then why are we still pretending we hate him?

My boots shuffled on the old wood floors of the headmaster's residence as I passed dark window after dark window on my way down the hall. The house was situated behind the dorms and surrounded by trees, as if the encroaching forest wanted to swallow it whole, and it seemed as ancient as the forest too, with its stained glass windows and dark wood paneling and tiny fireplaces in every room. Whereas the Pembroke campus was all New England charm, the headmaster's house had more of a *Turn of the Screw* vibe—a little creepy, a lot creaky, and very cool.

Except, of course, if you were trying to get down the noisy Victorian-era staircase for a midnight snack. Then all the creakiness and creepiness were suddenly a lot less amusing.

I got to my room and quietly closed the door—even though slamming it would've felt really good right about now—and took a look around. It looked the same as it did before I went to the party. Before I once again fell into the logic-abyss that seemed to be Keaton Constantine. Before I let Keaton give me an orgasm —*again*.

Frustrated, I tossed my bag on my bed and then sat at my desk.

I knew I had the other applications to the other schools that were on my parents' hit list. The problem was I had zero motivation to apply to those, not even to add to my pile of safeties. Instead, there was the one that I wanted, and the even earlier escape it was promising through the pre-degree program.

What if you don't get in? What if they reject you?

The seeds of doubt were right there in my gut along with the seeds of discontent. The doubt had this gray smoky flavor to it. Hard to pinpoint, hard to make dissipate.

I pushed aside the Harvard, Brown, and Dartmouth applications, and I pulled out my letter for the Sorbonne program instead. And then I cracked open my laptop to the tab I'd had open on my browser since I'd gotten the letter.

The online application for the program was already done. Complete, ready. All I had to do was hit *submit*. But for over a week I'd been unable to do it. Unable to just pull the fucking trigger.

My father's lecture reverberated in my head.

Get your act together, that lecture said. *Be what we need you to be.*

Keaton's words came rushing back to me too.

Are you always going to be what everyone else wants you to be? Or are you going to do what might actually make you happy?

I didn't even need to think about it anymore. I knew what I wanted. I clicked *submit*.

The Sorbonne. Photography. An early escape. The last thing on earth my parents would ever approve of.

But it was the first thing I'd done in months that felt entirely like me.

"You can't stay angry with me forever," I said, watching Iris stare determinedly out my car window. Outside the car, there were trees and trees and trees, heavy with leaves that were newly flushed with fall. You'd think we were still in Vermont with all this foliage, but no, we were driving through Yonkers, which meant we'd been in the car for four hours.

Four *long* hours.

Four hours of Iris pretending I barely existed, four hours of her answering all my questions with one-word answers. Four hours of her glaring at me when I nudged her knee or brushed against her hand.

Actually, the entire past week and a half had been strained between us, which was not great timing because it had finally come time to take the pictures that would eventually turn into our project, and we needed to cooperate now more than ever.

We'd both managed to agree that we wanted to get away from Vermont to get our images at least. Everyone else was doing trees and mountains and lakes, and I'd turned to her during our last session and said, "I want to do the city."

Because fuck that trite bucolic crap. Any idiot with a cell phone could take a picture of some trees, dial up the contrast, and then write a douchey exhibit label for it. But Iris and I weren't idiots. We were better than the obvious answer. And what was less obvious for a landscape than a city?

Iris had immediately seen the appeal, dropping her cold shoulder act to look at me with a thoughtful expression. "Skyscrapers instead of woods. Streets instead of rivers. I can see that."

"We could contrast it with what a typical landscape is expected to be," I'd said, tapping my pencil against the table we were sitting at. "I could integrate some illustrated landscape shit between buildings or on top of them. On the sides. Rooftop farms, you know, like a solarpunk feel . . ."

Iris had shaken her head. "Too futuristic."

"It's conceptual," I'd defended.

"It's season three *Westworld*. It's Wakanda. It's *Zootopia*. It's been done."

"Yeah, it has. Because it's fucking cool."

She'd narrowed her eyes at me. She'd been pissed since that night in the woods when I'd dry-fucked her to orgasm and then called her "bait" ten minutes after, and it seemed like she took a particular, resentful delight in saying, "It's *fan art*, Keaton. Is that really what you want your semester project to be? Fan art?"

"Fan art is badass stuff. Don't be such a fucking snob."

Her eyebrow had arched. And then she'd continued on like I hadn't spoken at all. "We'll do a fake double exposure. One of the city, one of the landscape it would have been if it had never been developed."

I'd considered it a moment. It wasn't a terrible idea, and as much as I'd like to get her to admit that my idea was cooler, I couldn't deny that her vision was probably more reflective.

And *reflective* was the kind of shit that got top marks and written up in the local papers, which I wasn't about to say no to.

So Iris's idea it was.

And now here we were, using my family's car and driver to get us to the city, planning on staying at the Constantine penthouse while we worked since my mom was currently in Bishop's Landing and we'd have it all to ourselves. I'd pitched staying at my place to Iris as a way for her to save money on splitting a hotel room and as the option that made the most logical sense—but I'd be lying if I said I hadn't thought about her swimming naked in my family's rooftop pool. Showering in *my* shower. Sleeping in *my* bed.

I'd be lying if I said I hadn't thought of all those things constantly.

God, I wanted her again. I wanted to kiss her so badly that sometimes I caught myself licking my own teeth. I wanted my fingers back in her panties so terribly that I had to curl them into fists to keep from grabbing her.

I wanted to nudge those thighs apart and show her everything I could do, everything I could make her feel.

I just wanted *her*.

The good news was that we had a pretty good track record when it came to fooling around when she was pissed at me. And with that comforting thought, I crossed my arms and leaned back in my seat, giving her my smirkiest smirk.

She very pointedly didn't look at me, but I knew she could feel my stare heating against her face. She frowned out the window.

"So does your dad know that you're spending a weekend in the city?" I asked. "With me?"

She sighed. "No, of course not."

"It's for school, Big Red. I figured he'd understand."

She cut a look at me that very clearly said, *I know you are trying to irritate me and it's working.*

Unfortunately for her, I knew the secret. And the secret was that a provoked Iris was a horny Iris.

Not exactly incentive to stop.

"And I'm sure your father wouldn't have minded that you'd be staying at my place," I teased. I let a hand trace an idle circle on her knee, just below the hem of her uniform skirt.

She shivered a little, but she didn't stop me.

"And he wouldn't have minded knowing you'd be in my bed. Wearing something cute. Needing kissed good night."

"Keaton," she scolded. Her eyes were on the driver's partition in front of us.

I circled her knee again, a bit higher this time, flirting with the bottom of her skirt. "He can't hear or see us."

"It's still not right," she protested. Although her objection wasn't very convincing when she was also parting her legs the tiniest bit, like she couldn't help but want me between them.

"Tell me where your parents think you are," I persuaded, letting my fingers drift higher. I was caressing the soft skin of her inner thigh now. It wouldn't be much longer until I felt cotton.

God, I was hard just thinking about it. Hard thinking about *plain, cotton panties.*

I was good and fucked for this girl, and she had no fucking clue.

"They think I'm with Serafina," she finally admitted, and when I rewarded her with a graze of my fingertips right over her cotton-covered core, she instinctively arched against my touch. "On—on a campus visit to Columbia."

She was breathless now. I stroked her again and grinned evilly as she mewled and shivered, now shamelessly spreading her legs.

"There. That wasn't so hard now, was it?"

"You're cheating."

I plucked teasingly at the edge of the cotton, so close to her heat. "I had to, Briggs. You weren't playing fair."

"You weren't playing fair when you accused me of being bait."

"*Aha*," I crowed softly. "I knew you were upset about that."

"Of course I was—" Her voice broke off as I slid a finger between her panties and her skin and caressed her there.

"I'm sorry I said it," I told her. "I shouldn't have."

The pad of my index finger found her clit and I started working it in small, light strokes.

"It's okay," she said, her eyes fluttering closed. "I forgive you."

"Huh. That was easy."

She opened her eyes to look at me again. It wasn't a glare this time, or even one of her suspicious sidelong glances. This time, she looked at me like she wanted to spend the rest of her life with her mouth on mine.

"You make me forget why things should be hard," she said, and then her hand slipped down to cover my own.

Together we pushed my finger inside her sheath. I hissed when I felt how wet she was. "Jesus Christ, Iris."

"I want to see you," she whispered, her eyes dipping down to where my cock was currently trying to drill a hole through my pants. "I still haven't seen you."

I was ready to do it, ready to give her whatever she wanted, if only it meant I could keep my finger inside her, when I looked out the windows and realized we were on Park Avenue, and almost in front of my building.

I pulled my fingers free and sucked them clean, wishing I could take a video of her watching me as I did it. Because with her eyes like this—dark and glazed with desire—with her full pink lips parted and her cheeks flushed under all those freckles—she was the sexiest thing in the entire goddamn world.

"We're going to finish this," I promised her in a growl as the car rolled to a stop.

She made no move to close her thighs, and her hand made a naughty movement downward, like she was going to finish it by herself if she had to.

I caught her wrist. "Uh-uh, sweetheart. As much as I need to watch you get yourself off, it's not going to be where I can't savor it."

"And why can't you savor it right now?" she asked, squirming and squirming with her uniform skirt pushed high up on her thighs. My erection surged, and for a moment, I nearly said *fuck it,* and gave in. Fingering her while I jerked off suddenly felt as necessary as breathing.

Think of the pool, Constantine. Think of her all adorable and whimpering in your bed.

With superhuman strength, I clawed back my control and smoothed her skirt back over her thighs as the doorman opened my door.

"Because we're here."

"Wow," Iris said, spinning in yet another circle. "Wow *wow* wow."

"It's a good thing you want to go to Paris, Big Red, because you seem to only know one word in English."

She flipped me off, but kept spinning, eventually spinning her way out to the rooftop terrace, which had a northern panoramic view of the city, including the Chrysler Building and the Empire State Building. It also had a private heated pool and lots of big outdoor couches and beds at the side—perfect for kissing and petting while the city lights glowed around us. It might get chilly, though, so I'd need to grab a blanket to wrap Iris in . . .

I followed her onto the terrace, shaking my head at myself.

Since when had I become that guy? Blankets-so-a-girl-wouldn't-get-cold guy?

I wasn't an asshole—at least, I wasn't a *super*-asshole—and I was always good to the girls I was with. I just couldn't remember the last time it had occurred to me to be chivalrous. To make sure the girl I was with didn't just leave with a satisfied body, but a happy heart too.

Iris stopped spinning and smiled at me, the wind ruffling her bright hair all around her face. Her blue eyes were the same color as the autumn sky, and a dimple was denting her cheek, and she was so gorgeous, so sexy, that I couldn't stand not to be touching her for a single moment longer.

"I need to thank your mom for letting us stay here," she was saying as I was striding towards her, my hands already itching to grab her and haul her close. "I'll have to thank her at Parents' Weekend next week."

I seized her by the arm and drew her into me. "You'll have to settle for a note, Big Red. She never comes to Parents' Weekend."

"Never?" She looked surprised as I slid a hand into her perfect hair and then tightened the tiniest bit. Her eyelids fluttered in pleasure as I did it again.

It made me want to growl in satisfaction. I knew she liked me bossy, I knew she liked me a little rough, but god, to see it out here in broad daylight and without me warming her up for it first . . .

I needed to taste her again.

Now.

I tugged her head to the side to open up her neck to me. "Never," I confirmed for her as I started kissing along her jaw and throat. "She usually can't be bothered. My other siblings take up most of her time."

"But why?" she asked, sounding confused. "You do all the right things. The grades, the rugby. The girlfriend . . ."

And at the mention of Clara, I felt her stiffen under my kisses and start to pull away.

Shit.

"Every time," Iris said, almost to herself. "Every fucking time. I say I'm not going to let you get to me, I'm going to keep my distance because you have a girl-friend, and yet—"

I couldn't let her pull away. I couldn't let her go another minute without knowing that I was fucking obsessed with her and nothing else mattered but us.

Sorry, Clara.

"She's not really my girlfriend," I confessed.

It felt strange to say it aloud, finally, after all this time—I felt both heavier and lighter all at once.

"We aren't dating, we aren't in love, we don't fuck. We are nothing, Iris. She and I are a lie."

I still had my hand in Iris's hair, and I guided her face to look up at mine. She blinked at me with so much wariness and hope and uncertainty in her autumn-sky eyes.

"But why would you pretend to date someone for this long?" she asked.

I let out a long breath. "My mother. She's close with Clara's parents. They've always seen us as a destined pair, I guess, since a Blair and a Constantine marriage would be good for both families."

Iris wrinkled her nose. It was unbearably cute. "Can't you just tell them that you're not interested in each other?"

"We've tried. But then Clara had to go and fall in love with a boy her parents would hate, and then us dating became a convenient cover for her. I became her alibi when she needed to sneak off to see her real boyfriend, and she became a way to keep my mother happy with me. Well, maybe not happy so much as 'less disappointed,' but you get the idea."

She stared up at me, searching my gaze. "So . . . you're not really dating Clara? She isn't really going to kill me for kissing you?"

"She might be pissed that you're blowing her cover, but that's all."

She pulled her bottom lip between her teeth.

My cock responded like she'd shoved her hand in my pants, and I dropped my forehead to hers, closing my eyes. "Let me kiss you again," I said. Begged. "Let me taste you."

"Is that . . . is that all you want to do?" she asked. Her voice was strange. Not hesitant exactly, but more like—more like shy. Like she wanted to ask for something but didn't know how.

I opened my eyes. "Babe, you can't expect me to answer that honestly."

"Why not?"

Why not? Because I had an entire folder in my brain full of fantasies and scenarios so filthy they'd send her running. Because *all I want to do* had a very easy and short answer.

Everything.

I wanted to do everything with her.

I wanted time to stop and the world to freeze, and then I wanted to fuck her in every position I knew of and some that hadn't even been invented yet. I wanted to finger her in public, I wanted to eat her out while she looked at the stars. I wanted to come all over those freckled tits.

I wanted to make her climax so many times that she'd be as obsessed with me as I was with her.

"Keaton," she said, sliding her hands up to my face. "Tell me what you're thinking."

I leaned down and nipped her lower lip. "No way."

She did the thing again, where she ran her fingers through the place where my hair curled behind my ears. It sent hot, shivering thrills all over me. "Then show me," she whispered. "Show me everything you want to do to me."

I pulled back. The breeze ruffled between us as I studied her face.

"You sure?"

She blushed. "Yes."

I palmed her hips, pulling her lower half tight against mine. My thick erection dug into the softness of her belly. I wanted to fuck her. I wanted to go through an entire box of condoms with her.

But I also needed her to be sure.

"You know me," I told her. "I'm not the hearts-and-flowers type. I'll make it good for you, but I can't promise it will be sweet."

She pushed back against me, licking her lips. "Keaton," she said, her fingers brushing the hair behind my ears.

"Yeah?"

"Shut up."

I laughed as I kissed her again, sliding my hands around to cup her bottom and then lift her into my arms. She wrapped her legs around my waist, and I carried her back inside the penthouse, kissing her the whole way.

"*Y*ou're a giant," she told me between kisses.

My chest swelled a little. Working out meant I slayed on the field, yes, but being able to sweep Iris off to my bed like this was pure magic. I'd endure Coach's brutal conditioning every single day for the rest of my life if it meant being able to kiss her while I carried her off to be fucked.

"You're just tiny," I said, but I couldn't hide the smugness in my tone.

"More like you're just full of yourself," she teased back, but she didn't sound upset.

I bit her jaw as we walked past the kitchen island. "You're about to be full of myself too."

She groaned, and I stopped walking, because I needed to touch her again, I needed to taste her again. *Right now*.

I set her on the counter, my hands already diving under her skirt to pull off her panties. I worked them off her hips and legs, stuffing them in my pocket. Like hell was she getting those back.

"Hold up your skirt and spread your legs," I told her as I got to my knees. I was just tall enough that when I knelt, her pussy was right where I wanted it. And so, when she finally did as I asked and pulled up her skirt, I was presented with a view that would keep my right hand busy for years.

I'd been able to glimpse her before, in the moonlight, but it was nothing like this. Nothing like being able to see her in broad daylight. Nothing like seeing where she was pink and slick and ready for me. Nothing like being able to see her silky, scarlet curls. Yes, it was a stereotype that guys love redheaded pussy, and yes, it was still hot as hell, stereotype or not.

I didn't warm her up. I didn't kiss my way up her thigh. I didn't give her chaste, closed-mouth kisses against her seam. Instead, I dove in like a starving man and clamped my hands over her hips to keep her still as I stroked into her with my tongue.

"Fuck, babe," I murmured into her, barely able to stop devouring her in order to get the words out. "You taste so good." Even better than I remembered. Even better than I'd dreamed.

She was so sweet here, so very *Iris*—and it was a taste I was worried I'd never get enough of, given the rock-hard state of my dick.

She tried to arch as my tongue flicked over her clit, but I wouldn't let her. I held her fast and started going in earnest—fluttering, caressing, sucking—full on burying my face into her. My nose was in her curls and my lips were wet with her, and when I chanced a look up at her, she was already looking down at me with a look that fired my blood right up.

She was looking at me like I was some kind of king.

Like I was some kind of idol.

"Keaton," she whispered.

"Keep still and keep that skirt up," I ordered, going in again, abandoning myself to every dirty kiss and lick I'd fantasized about giving this pretty ginger pussy. She was so soft and so warm here.

She was heaven, and I was going to give her heaven in return.

I carefully worked a single finger inside, keeping my mouth at the swollen bud above her opening, feeling her thighs tense around my head. She was getting close, her body practically thrumming as she got wetter and tighter—and wetter and tighter still.

Fuck. I'd jerked off to the thought of this so many times, it was nearly impossible to keep myself from reaching down and freeing my cock, like a perverted Pavlovian response to having my mouth between her legs.

Soon, I promised my aching erection. *So soon*.

But Iris first.

I used my free hand to hold her hip even tighter—and just in time, too, because as her climax broke against my mouth, she sank her fingers into my hair and rocked against me, trembling so hard I wondered if she'd tremble right off the edge of the counter. I wondered if I'd have to catch her and then lay her down right there on my kitchen floor and sink into her slick warmth.

Because if she literally fell off the counter because I made her come so hard, there was no way I was making it all the way to my bed. No fucking way.

Luckily for us both, I managed to keep her braced up on her perch while I finished the job, making sure to kiss her pussy through every last flutter and squeeze. And then when she was all done, I withdrew my finger and stood, scooping her into my arms without a word.

"Keaton," she sighed dreamily, resting her head against my shoulder.

"You're always so sweet after you come for me."

"Is that why you do it?" she asked, her tone half drowsy, half teasing. "So I'll be nice?"

I smirked down at her. "I like it when you're mouthy too, you know."

"Oh, is that so?"

We were in my room now, and thank God, because I was so hard I could feel my heartbeat in my dick. Need for her had bunched itself into a hot ball at the base of my spine, and the pressure was painful, threatening to snap my resolve.

"You know it is," I told her as I set her on my bed and then crawled over her. The light was slowly fading into the lavender light of evening, and my big shadow dwarfed her small frame on the bed. "Whenever we fight, I end up begging to put my mouth on you."

She gave me a doubtful look. "I'd say you're more *bossy* than *begging*."

"I don't know what you're talking about. Now, take off your shirt."

She rolled her eyes at me but smiled to herself all the same as she pulled off her sweater and then started unbuttoning the white shirt underneath. I mirrored her as I rose up to my knees, opening my shirt and then tearing it off. I kicked off my shoes and pants, wearing nothing but boxer briefs as I palmed my erection and looked down at the living wet dream in my bed.

She was in nothing but her bra and her skirt now, and when she parted her legs, it was obvious there was nothing underneath. Nothing between my hot gaze and her waiting pussy.

"Bra off," I said hoarsely. "I want to be able to suck on your tits."

The smile on her face turned into an expression so hungry I nearly came in my boxer briefs. "Oh, really," she said softly. She reached behind her back, and in a few seconds, I could see her perfect breasts—pert and freckled and tipped with nipples already straining to be sucked on. "I think I want that too."

She gathered her skirt up in her fingers, pulling the hem all the way up past her naked pussy.

"I think I want everything," she whispered.

Looking at her made me feel like I'd been kicked in the chest. Those sweet tits, her soft stomach, that place between her legs that I could still taste on my lips . . .

Those bright blue eyes, looking up at me with hunger and trust, and still glazed with satisfaction from the orgasm I just gave her . . .

And her hair, all flame-colored satin, tousled over my pillow as it should fucking be. Her hair should be spilled over my pillow every night for the next eight months. For the next million months.

I could barely fucking stand it, how good and right it was to have her like this.

Once I could breathe again, I reached over to my end table and pulled a condom from the drawer, tearing the packet open with my teeth.

"You've done this before, Big Red?" I asked as I tugged my boxer briefs down and rolled the condom over my thick length.

I figured she probably hadn't; she'd had *virgin* written all over her from the start. And normally I didn't care about that kind of caveman shit—sex was sex, didn't matter if it was the first time or the ninetieth—but it did matter that we went at the right pace.

Her eyes were hot on my dick as I worked the latex down. A flush was working its way up from her chest to her neck. "No," she murmured. "This is—you're my first."

It shouldn't matter, I told myself again. It *didn't* matter.

But that she was trusting me with this—trusting me to make it good for her—it made something behind my ribs go tight and sharp.

"I promise you won't regret it," I swore, leaning back over her. I kissed her thoroughly as I reached down to sweep the head of my cock through her seam, rubbing her up and down with my tip until she started moving underneath me and chasing it.

I kissed her neck and then a soft breast as I finally nudged myself inside—just the tiniest amount. Just the tip.

I held my breath. Christ she was tight. And warm. And so slippery wet. She stiffened underneath me, pulling in a breath, and I bent to take a taut nipple into my mouth, sucking and working it until she relaxed again.

And then I pushed in.

Not much—just an inch—but it was enough to send her hands flying to my shoulders. Her eyes were round when I looked down at her, and her lower lip was caught between her teeth.

I froze. "Does it hurt too much?" I asked. It was almost hurting *me*—she was that tight and warm inside. My balls were already drawing up to my body, eager to release into her, and I had to clench everything in my stomach and thighs and ass to keep from blowing my load right then and there.

She shook her head after a minute. "No. No, it feels better now." She ran her eyes down my chest and abdomen, her stare going dark with lust as she looked down at where my cock was wedged into her. "Just go slow if you can," she said in a husky voice.

"Anything," I promised her. "Anything you need." Although going slow felt like a Herculean task right now. Everything in my body was screaming to thrust, to rut, to pump into her until I exploded.

I reached down to gently massage her clit as I pushed in a little bit more, my entire body trembling with the restraint.

"God," she breathed. "It's—it's so much. Are you all the way in yet?"

I almost laughed, and the noise came out pained. Nearly animal-like. "No, babe. Not even halfway."

"*How?*"

I bent down to suck on the firm berry of a nipple. "Because I'm big and you're tiny. Now, *shhh*. Let me make you feel good."

It was the hardest thing I'd ever done, working my way into her virgin slickness without losing control. There was no word for how that velvet grip felt around my dick, for how slick and hot she was, for the way her silken walls caressed me. I gritted my teeth, I clenched my jaw—I even closed my eyes so I wouldn't see all that fiery hair or those sweet, cinnamon freckles—and then somehow, miraculously, I made it all the way to the root without hurting her or embarrassing myself.

Once I was sunk to the hilt, I managed—with some deep breathing and counting backwards—to get a hold of myself enough that I could open my eyes and look down at her. When I did, I nearly regretted it, because she was so fucking beautiful like this, all flushed and flutter-eyed, her lips parted and her nipples still hard and begging for my mouth again.

I braced myself on one hand and started circling her needy clit with my thumb, not moving my hips at all. I just rubbed and circled with her impaled on me, and then bit by bit, little by little, she started to move. She started to fuck herself on my erection, chasing the pleasure, circling her hips and rocking against the pressure on her swollen bud.

"Oh god," she whispered, her hands pushing back into my hair and pulling tight. I hissed in response, only barely able to keep from coming then. "Oh god, Keaton —it's like—it feels so—"

What it felt like I never did learn, because she shattered beneath me with a long, delicious cry that had my hips churning between her thighs before I even realized what was happening. Her body went tight and quivery around me, squeezing me, milking me, and it was as if her body was trying to pull the orgasm right out of my cock, like it was yanking it clean out of my soul.

I fell over her, sliding my arms beneath her slender frame and giving her my weight as I gave in. All these weeks of wanting her, of needing her, of jerking off constantly because she made me crazed with lust—it all came out now, ripping through my body with the force of a storm. I buried my face in her hair and pumped the condom full of my orgasm, rocked to the core by each and every jolting pulse. Slain by every jagged surge of pleasure as I emptied my need into her body.

Wrecked with how beautiful she was, even now—sweaty and tousled and looking exactly like a girl who'd just been thoroughly fucked.

When the orgasm finally slowed and then abated, we shared a long, lazy kiss. And when I pulled away to take care of the condom, she murmured, "You did it, you know."

"Did what?"

She smiled a smile that could shame the sun. "You made it good for me."

My chest went all tight again, for reasons I didn't understand—or didn't want to understand. "Yeah?"

Then that smile turned incendiary, and she reached for me as I walked back from the small wastebasket by my desk. She licked her lips in a way that had me getting hard all over again. "Now, let me see if I can think of something to make good for you."

"Iris," I groaned, already climbing back on the bed, because—what, I'm going to say no?

"*Shh,*" she teased, getting up and crawling down my body. "Let me make you feel good."

And then her slender fingers were on me, and *good* was nowhere even close to how I felt.

"*D*o you think we've got enough?"

Keaton was scrolling through my camera as we stood on a sidewalk in Chinatown, combing through all the pictures we'd taken today. We'd snapped expansive views from the observation deck at 30 Rock; we'd captured the bustle and rush of Grand Central Terminal. We'd found Grove Court—the almost eerily out-of-time nook of ivy-covered, white-shuttered brick—and we'd gotten shots of the Brooklyn Bridge from every possible angle. We'd used up all that delicious autumn light, and now evening was creeping in, along with a stiff, chilly breeze.

"I think we've got everything we need," he said, lingering over a picture I'd taken from the observation deck this morning. I'd taken it right as the sun was breaking through a fluff of thick clouds, and it managed to catch the way its newly released rays broke over the skyline like gilded waves upon a jagged, glassy shore.

"This looks like something out of a movie," he said, grinning up at me. "You're brilliant, babe. I'm fucking an actual genius."

I grinned back, but the grin was short-lived.

The words *brilliant* and *genius* went down like compliments should—smooth and sweet.

But I had no idea how to parse my response to the last part. When he said the word *fucking* like that, rough and proud and suggestive all at once, I wanted to tackle him to the sidewalk and rip his pants off. But I also couldn't help the sharp stab in my chest at hearing it.

Was fucking all this was to him?

What else did you expect, Iris? Did you expect him to tell you he was in love with you?

No. *No.*

No, of course not. That would be both stupid and ridiculous, and I was neither. I knew sex didn't equal love. Even an idiot could see that Keaton Constantine wasn't the loving type—and I definitely wasn't in love with him, anyway. I mean, hell, hadn't I only just decided I didn't hate him? Of course I wasn't in love with him.

It's just . . . looking at him right now with that *grin* and that lock of hair falling over his forehead . . . feeling the tenderness between my legs and the flutter of my pulse at his nearness—I couldn't say that the idea of love sounded that awfully stupid. He was sexy and secretly talented, he was cocky and bossy and also the kind of guy that would do anything to help a friend.

Would it be so terrible? To fall in love with him?

It would if he didn't love you back.

Because that—it would break me.

Of that I had no doubt.

"I still can't believe this is your *home,*" I said as we walked back inside the Constantine penthouse. When we'd woken up this morning after having sex two more times last night, I'd demanded a tour—which he'd given and which also ended with us having sex on a rug in front of a fireplace faced with some fancy green marble imported from Italy.

It wasn't that I hadn't been in expensive houses before —attending boarding school and having boarding-school friends invariably meant staying over at places that were infinitely nicer than a headmaster's residence —but the Constantine penthouse was still far beyond anything I'd ever seen.

The huge windows looking out onto the city, and the soaring ceilings, and the glass and steel staircases that looked like works of art . . . it all screamed *money*. And not just any kind of money, but like, *big* money. Russian oligarch money. Own-multiple-private-islands money.

Keaton Constantine wasn't just the king of Pembroke.

When it came his time, he was going to be king of the world.

And it didn't do anything to make me feel better about where things stood between us. Why would a king want a freckled new girl with parental baggage? Of course he wouldn't.

And you don't want him either, remember? You're bound for Paris—the sex stuff is just a fun stop along the way.

"I can't believe I still haven't gotten to see you naked in my pool," Keaton said as he came up behind me and pulled me into his arms. He was hard again, and the rigid heft of his erection pressed into my backside like a luscious promise.

I should have been too tender to think about sex again, but when he nipped at my earlobe and slid a hand down to cup my pussy over my dress, my entire body went hot and shivery. The sore place between my legs ached for more.

I pushed into his touch, and he made a noise deep in his chest, like a growl. "You ready for more, baby?"

"How about," I said, looking at the darkened sky outside, "we try out your pool?"

His grip didn't loosen on me, like he was torn between fucking me bent over a nearby sofa or finally getting his Iris pool fantasy.

With a heavy breath, he finally released me.

"No clothes, Iris," he said huskily. "I want you bare."

God, when he used that voice . . . I quivered. It frightened me how much control he had over my body, over my reactions, just by being *him*. It frightened me to think he might have that kind of control over my heart —that he could set it to racing with happiness or thudding with anxious pain. I couldn't let that happen.

I wouldn't.

Resolved, I stepped away from him and cast a coy glance over my shoulder as I started walking towards the terrace, lit only by the glow of the city and the underwater lights set deep in the pool. I pulled off my dress as I walked. And then my bra. And then my panties. Until I was in nothing but goosebumps and the little ankle boots I'd worn around the city today.

Keaton prowled after me as I went, his eyes glittering in the shadows and his hands clenching into fists, as if to keep himself from grabbing me. I bent at the waist to unzip the little zippers on the boots, giving him a show, and when I stood back up with bare feet and glanced back at him, he looked downright *dangerous*.

"Careful, Iris," he warned.

I arched an eyebrow. "I thought you wanted me naked."

"I can't remember a single thought I've ever had," he said darkly, "when you bend over like that."

I gave him my naughtiest smile and then dove into the pool without another word. The water was warm—so much warmer than the fall air outside—and when I broke the surface, I could see little wisps of steam hovering over the pool like fog. Above me, stars twinkled, and all around the terrace, the city twinkled back.

The illicit feel of the water sliding over my pebbled nipples and past the exposed secrets between my legs hit me harder than liquor. And even more intoxicating were Keaton's eyes, glowing in the near-darkness as he sat on the edge of the pool. While I'd jumped in, he'd kicked off his shoes and socks too, rolling up his pant legs so he could sit with his feet in the water.

"You're not coming in here with me?" I asked, swimming up to him.

He leaned back on his hands, his eyes raking over my naked form. His voice was all hunger and stormy greed when he said, "No, Iris. I'm going to watch you swim for me."

I could see where his cock strained against his pants, but he made no move to touch it; he did nothing that would interrupt this visual feast for himself.

The intensity of his gaze was—heady.

Flattering.

So very easy to confuse with something more than lust.

I flipped over onto my back and kicked my way to the far edge of the pool, knowing he'd enjoy seeing my wet stomach and breasts as I did. When I got to the wall—which was made of thick glass and gave me a dizzying view down to the street far below—I asked him, "Do you make all the girls swim naked in your pool?"

"Just the bratty ones," he replied. His voice was low and soft—so soft I could barely hear him over the lap of the water and the whipping breeze. I turned to face him.

"So I'm not just the latest in a long line of naked pool nymphs?"

The corner of his mouth curved up. "Jealous, Iris?"

Yes, I wanted to say. The idea of another girl doing this with him, doing anything with him—it sent scalding knives of jealousy stabbing into my chest. And I hated it. I hated being jealous. It wasn't as if I hadn't crawled into his bed with my eyes wide open.

Okay, so I didn't so much *crawl* as I was scooped up and carried to his bed, but the point stands.

I knew what kind of guy he was. I knew I couldn't expect much.

Then why do you care so much about the other girls?

"Not jealous at all," I lied, pushing off the wall and swimming back to him. His eyes slid over me appreciatively as I cut through the water, his tongue slipping out to lick his lower lip. Like he was thinking about tasting me.

"You can rest easy," he said as I swam up to his feet. "You're the first girl I've ever brought here."

"Really?" I hated how happy that made me. I hated how happy I sounded about it.

Keaton nodded, and his expression had changed—less hunger, more inscrutability. I had no idea what he was thinking right now. "This place is full of memories for me. Some of them happy, and some of them not so happy. But even when it comes to the unhappy memories . . . I never wanted to bring someone inside my home unless they were worth it, if that makes sense. If I didn't feel like they could understand those memories. And me."

I could feel my cheeks glow with pleasure. He was saying that I was worth it. That he thought I understood him. Maybe even that he cared—

Don't get carried away.

I refused to fish for compliments, no matter how badly I wanted to, so I just wrapped my fingers around his ankles under the water. I was about to ask a follow-up question—not about me but his house and how long he'd lived here—when he said, "What about you, Briggs? Brought any boys back to the headmaster? Snuck someone into your twin bed and kissed them there?"

I gave a humorless laugh. "And reveal to my father that I do anything other than zealously prepare for college? No, I'm smarter than that."

"He wants you to go to an Ivy that badly, huh?"

Keaton didn't sound incredulous or disbelieving. He sounded like he understood. It truly was par for the course in our world.

The only difference between me and the other Pembroke students is that I had to get into my chosen school on merit alone, because I didn't have the guarantee of a legacy or money that could be conveniently endowed.

"Yes," I said. "It's all he wants from me."

"And you want to go to Paris instead," he stated. "And fall in love with a French guy."

He frowned rather adorably at that last part, and my heart gave a leap, before I pushed it firmly back down where it belonged. The frown wasn't because he was sad I might go somewhere else, and it wasn't because he was truly jealous. It was just caveman possessiveness, and while it was kind of hot, I was too smart to mistake it for anything more.

But I still found myself confessing, as if to reassure him. "The French guy is optional. The real reason I want to go to Paris is so I can attend the Sorbonne. To study photography."

I let go of his ankles, feeling suddenly awkward. I tried to swim away, but before I could, he reached down and snatched my wrist, pulling me between his legs so he could look at my face.

"So that's the real reason for Paris," he said softly. "Not for some European guy or for petit fours at a cafe, but to follow your heart."

When he said it like that, I felt a little embarrassed. Embarrassed that I had such an earnest, pie-in-the-sky dream. Embarrassed that I was that easy to read.

"I mean, the petit fours and the European guy are still *part* of it," I joked weakly.

His gaze was so intense right now, so penetrating, and I wondered if this was what his opponents saw on the rugby field. This stare that allowed me no secrets, no quarter. This stare that said *you, and everything you hold dear, is about to be mine.*

It made fresh goosebumps prickle all over my skin. It made heat pool low, low in my belly.

"Don't hide from me, Iris," he said finally.

"I'm not—"

Abruptly, I was hauled from the water—first by my wrists and then by his large hands firmly under my arms—and then with no effort at all, he lifted me in his arms as he got to his feet. Once again, I realized how massive he was, how powerfully built, and my toes curled with lust as I realized he was using all that power to sweep me off somewhere to have his way with me.

"Joking about what you really want is hiding," he said as he carried me inside. "We've been real with each other from the start. We're not going to stop now."

15

$\mathcal{W}$e were close to his bedroom, but he walked right past the door to the adjoining door, which opened up into a spacious bathroom with a freestanding marble bathtub and a glassed-in shower the size of a small principality. He set me carefully on my feet, and then tugged off his shirt—slowly enough for me to appreciate the flex and play of the muscles banding his lean abdomen and broad chest.

"Well, Briggs?" he asked, starting in on his jeans. I had no idea why it was so sexy to watch him as he popped open the button of his fly and tugged down the zipper, but it was. I felt like I was being hypnotized by the subtle flex of the muscles in his forearm. By the vein tracing along the back of his hand. By the slow revelation of his lower abs, with their dark trail of hair leading deeper into his jeans.

"Briggs," he prompted, sounding amused. "I'm up here."

"Sorry," I breathed, not sorry at all. He had me naked and dripping in his bathroom—what else did he expect?

"I want to know if you're going to be real with me," he said, kicking off his jeans. "No hiding. Just *us*."

He walked forward, his erection yet another display of shameless male power. It was big and thick and dark, framed between his narrow hips and those giant, rugby-playing thighs.

"No hiding," I said. "What does that mean?"

"It means no pretending like you do for the world. You want something? Own it."

A smile pulled at my mouth. "I want you."

His eyes hooded, and without breaking eye contact with me, he reached out and slid something off the bathroom counter. A condom.

"Is that so, Big Red? What else do you want?"

I could feel the flush starting on my chest, I could feel how my nipples drew even harder. "I want you inside me again."

He tore the packet open with his teeth, and within seconds, his proud erection was sheathed in clear latex. He gave himself an idle stroke as he stalked towards me, backing me towards the shower. "Inside your pussy, Iris? Fucking that sweet, tight place so deep that you're standing on your tiptoes while you beg to come?"

Guh.

Was it possible to have a heart attack from being too turned on?

"Yes," I whispered, stepping backwards into the shower. "That's what I want."

He reached past me. With a few deft movements, he had the water turned on, warm and already starting to fill the shower with steam, and then he spun me to face the wall.

"Hands here," he murmured, guiding my hands to the wall so that I was braced against it. The water fell hot and pleasant against our sides as he pressed his giant foot to mine and nudged it to the side so my legs were spread. He stepped between them with a satisfied noise that had my core fluttering in response.

"You still sore?" he asked as one big hand found my breast and kneaded it.

"A little," I admitted.

His other hand slid around my hip to circle my clit. "Tell me if it hurts," he whispered, and rubbed me so exquisitely that I couldn't even remember what hurting felt like. He waited until I was arching against his touch and panting into the steam before he notched the plump head of his cock at my entrance. And slowly —so slowly that I could feel every thick inch of him as he pushed in—he slid home with a muttered *Jesus*.

"It's so deep like this," I moaned, pressing my forehead to the shower wall. There was a tiny bit of soreness and sting with the intrusion, but it was nothing compared to the building knot of pleasure currently cinching between my legs. And when he answered me by thrusting again and doing what he promised—pushing me up to my tiptoes—I needed the wall more than ever.

"Fuck," I whimpered, and then whimpered again when he reached down and gave my clit what it needed.

He bent his head and bit my neck as he began pumping between my legs and giving me all the desire that had been coiling inside him since we first left the penthouse this morning. Every dark promise he'd made, every sultry look he'd given me—he was settling up now, demanding payment from my body. And not just with his pleasure, but my own too. Because the minute I broke apart around him, he followed, surging heavy into my body with a delicious growl, and before I had time to catch my breath, he was on his knees, stripping off the condom and sealing his mouth between my legs.

He ate me like that—him on his knees behind me—my hands still braced against the wall, and he spared no amount of filth. He licked where he shouldn't. He fucked my entrance with his tongue. His fingers worked me as he reached down with his free hand and jerked off.

And after we both came a second time—me against his mouth and him with hot ropes of seed between my feet —and I slumped to the shower floor next to him, he asked me again.

"What else do you want?"

I only had one answer, and it was the same one from yesterday.

"Everything."

I *was* sore the next day, but it was the kind of soreness that felt good. Like the sting after a giggling belly flop into a pool. Like the ache of a muscle well used.

And the way Keaton looked at me as his car pulled away from the Park Avenue curb and we started back towards Pembroke—god, that *look*. He looked at me like he was a conqueror and I was the fresh, green country he was about to claim.

But I also couldn't help the doubt that slithered through my thoughts. Of course we'd have a weekend of secrets and orgasms in the magic tower of his penthouse, but now that we were coming back to real life? To the world of gossip and grades and bonfire parties and my status as the headmaster's daughter?

What then?

I looked over at Keaton, who pulled my feet into his lap the moment the car started and was now stroking up my bare legs with greedy fingertips. "Are we—do you want to—" I cleared my throat, feeling awkward and needy and repugnantly anxious. "Are we going to do this again sometime?"

His hands went still on my legs, and when he looked over at me, that lock of hair was hanging over his forehead, like he was a cartoon fairy-tale prince made real. "Tell me what you mean by *this*, Iris. A trip to New York? Staying at my place?"

I was already shaking my head, even though I wouldn't say no to either opportunity if they arose again. "I mean us spending time together, Keaton. The hanging out. The fooling around. When we get to Pembroke, are we going to pretend this weekend never happened?"

Now all of him was completely still. Tense. I couldn't read his expression when he said, "Is that what you want? To stop?"

An instinctive pain welled up inside me at the very thought of stopping. And then a wave of fear followed that pain. If I was this far gone for him after only a weekend, what would happen after weeks of this at school? Months? I'd be broken over him. He'd break me, and then I'd just be the stupid girl who fell for the king of the school. The girl that fell for the rugby idol and his arrogant smirk.

No better than a fool.

"I don't know," I whispered, looking away. "I don't know what I want."

He didn't seem to like that answer at all. My seatbelt was unbuckled and I was in his lap before I could blink. He yanked me to his chest with one burly arm while his other hand slid up my skirt. Not to toy with me or tease, but to cup me. Hard. And with his hand molded possessively over me, he said in a fierce, rough voice, "Don't keep me from this. Don't keep *us* from this."

I couldn't help how I reacted to his touch. Just like in the library that very first time, his breathtaking arrogance only fired me—and my half-glaring, half-aroused response only stoked his need higher. He curled his hand over me even tighter, sending quivering heat to the place that needed his touch the most.

Focus, Iris!

"What about Clara?" I demanded, scowling at him.

He looked confused. "What about her?"

"We can't be having sex while everyone thinks you're with her!"

Keaton's brow wrinkled. It made him look unfairly cute. "Why not? She's got nothing to do with us."

My stomach knifed. "So you're just going to continue dating her," I said dully. "While you fuck me on the side."

"Iris," Keaton said, the arm around my waist now moving up my back. He buried his fingers in the wavy mass of my hair. "You're making this sound worse than it is. She and I don't fuck, we don't fool around, we don't even kiss, and you know why? Because I only kiss the girls I want."

I blinked at him.

I didn't want this ugly doubt nestled inside me. I didn't want what we'd shared this weekend to end up poisoned and ruined. I wanted to believe him. I wanted to imagine that the next few months or longer would be full of the same heady, thrilling fun we'd had this weekend.

A long minute passed while I thought. "Are you saying you don't want her?" I asked shyly. A little miserably.

Blue eyes searched my own as his hand tightened in my hair. "I want *you*," Keaton swore. "Your body. Your mouth. Your sass when we argue." He pressed his hips up underneath my bottom so I could feel exactly how much and how hard he wanted. "You're the one who's tied me up in fucking knots for weeks, and you're the one I can't stop thinking about, can't stop jerking off to, can't stop touching. Clara and I are playing a part. But you and me?" He let out a low, rough exhale. "We're the real fucking deal, Briggs."

As declarations went, it wasn't exactly Jane Austen-worthy. He didn't love me. He wasn't even willing to give up his fake relationship for me. He wanted to fuck me in secret, and that wasn't exactly a happily ever after.

But there was no mistaking the earnest ferociousness in his gaze, nor the colossal erection underneath me. And I wanted to believe him, I wanted to believe that he could chastely play his part with Clara and save all his desire for me.

God, how I wanted to believe it.

I pressed my hand to his sharp, sculpted jaw and pressed my forehead to his.

"You better mean that, Keaton," I whispered. "No wanting her. No touching her. No kissing her. You have to promise."

"I promise," he said seriously. "You and I together? We're real. Clara and me? We're fake as fake can be. You'll see for yourself when we get back."

I hoped so.

And I threw myself into that hope like a thrill seeker throwing themselves off a sea cliff into the waves, praying the whole time they didn't die on hidden rocks below, but also laughing with sheer adrenaline the whole way down.

I kissed him, and he kissed me back, his fingers finally nudging beneath my panties while he ducked his head to suck on my neck. And then I was lost to him the entire way back to school.

*N*early a week later, I woke up thinking of Iris, just as I had every damn morning since I met her.

With a groan, I rolled over and grabbed my phone to send her a quick text.

Keaton: I woke up thinking of you.

Iris: ☺ I woke up thinking about you too.

That warmth in my chest spread out to my extremities. God, is this what it felt like? To really care about someone and have them care about you back? It had been so long for me. Maybe never. With Iris, I felt like myself. Like I belonged somewhere. This girl owned me, and she had no idea.

I was already making plans. There were plenty of design schools in Paris. I was a little late to get a portfolio together but given the money I'd have access to after graduation, I could make anything happen. I knew how important Paris was to her. I had no set plans, so I could try Paris. I loved the city. And any city with Iris in it was one I could stay in for a while.

Keaton: Meet me by the Giant Oak? We'll have a picnic away from the prying eyes.

Iris: Keaton Constantine, well, aren't you romantic?

Keaton: I plan to try to feel you up in the great outdoors.

Iris: LOL, you're ridiculous.

I wasn't sure why she thought I was joking, but if I would get to see her and make her smile, I would take it.

Keaton: I'm only half kidding. But I can't wait to see you smile.

She sent a photo of her looking sleepy and bed rumpled with a huge smile on her face.

Keaton: Day made.

I pushed out of bed, still bleary-eyed, grabbed some clothes and a towel, and headed towards the bathroom when my phone buzzed again. Like the completely pussy-whipped jackass that I was, I ran to grab it. Because what if she sent me another kind of photo entirely?

Sure, you tell yourself that. Mostly, knowing she could have texted you just makes you smile.

Yeah, it did. And it was alarming. When I picked it up with a shit-eating grin on my face, I paused when I saw who it was. My mother.

Mom Monster: I've decided to come to campus after all today for Parents' Weekend. I'll meet you for lunch with Clara and her parents.

What the fuck?

Could I get away with pretending I hadn't seen it?

Mom Monster: Also, I can see you've read this. So acknowledge.

Fuck read receipts. There's nothing more passive-aggressive to my mother than reading a message and not replying immediately.

Keaton: Sorry, Mom. Busy.

Lies.

Mom Monster: I'm here. It is Parents' Weekend, so I know there's no games or practices, and there's nothing else on your agenda. I'll see you at 12:30.

Fuck. I didn't even bother with texting. Instead I picked up the phone and called Clara. "What the hell?"

She groaned. "You got the text too."

"Yeah, what the fuck? I had plans today."

She paused for a moment. "With the new girl?"

"She's none of your business," I said—politely but also firmly. I knew she'd been on Iris's case and that was stopping right now. "And make sure she stays that way. No more threats, okay?"

"Okay, okay. Sorry. I was just trying to keep up the front, you know? And she didn't even seem like your type."

"And who is? You?"

"Harsh much?"

I groaned and ran a hand through my hair. "Sorry. You're not the enemy, *they* are."

"Tell me about it. I was supposed to see Charlie. He got into Duke. So as luck would have it, we'll be at school together next year." She sounded so happy. That kind of elation was unusual for her. But she was always that happy when she talked about him.

"Congrats. I am happy for you."

There was another beat of silence. "Did you just express emotion and empathetic joy for another person?"

"Don't get too excited."

"Wow, new girl—sorry—Iris is good for you then. You seem almost happy too."

"Well, I'm not happy about today. What are we going to do?"

"I don't think we have any choice. We have to go."

"But I don't want to."

She sighed, "Keaton, all you have wanted all this time is for your mother to pay attention to you. To show up for you. She's doing that. I'm sure Iris will understand."

That was just the thing. Iris *would* understand. But I didn't. I didn't want to go. But I couldn't deny that little ball of light at the idea that my mother had come. For Parents' Weekend. And I hadn't even asked.

"Yeah, okay, that's a good point."

"Look, I know our parents aren't really the ones to give us hope and shit. But maybe this is good. I mean my parents always come, so I'm just praying that with your mother there they're not going to harangue me about my choice to go to Duke—if I get in, obviously—and not Harvard."

"Duke's at least still a good school though."

"Yeah, but it's not prestigious enough for Mommy."

"Well, good thing you have your own trust fund and you don't have to listen to her."

"Thank God for little miracles."

"Look, I'll see you at 12:30, yeah?"

I hung up with Clara while trying to figure out what the hell I was going to say to Iris. But in the end, all I could do was tell her the truth. She picked up on the first ring. "Hey. Are you about to get in the shower thinking about me?"

The smile pulled at my lips, and I couldn't help it. "I had been thinking about that shower in New York."

"Me too. So how does this work? Why isn't this video? It's a lot better if I can see you touching yourself."

I coughed a laugh. I had created a monster. "Actually, there's a change of plan today. I'm really sorry." I wasn't used to apologizing. Usually people apologized to me. While I withheld emotion one way or another.

"Oh, what's up?"

"My mother showed up."

There was a beat of silence. "Your mother?"

"Yeah, I know. Shocking right?"

"Hell yeah. But that's actually a big deal."

I sighed. "Yeah, that's what Clara said."

This time there was a longer pause. "Clara?"

Fuck. Should not have said that. "Yeah, my mom is insisting on lunch with her family. So I called her to find out if we could weasel out."

"Oh."

That one word carried the weight of so many sentences. So many orations. A whole goddamn Julius Caesar speech. Just with an *oh*.

"You know it's not like that."

"No, I know. I just still hate that you get to spend the afternoon with her. And not with me."

"Trust me, I'd rather be spending it with you." And that was the truth. I wanted to spend every moment with her. We luckily had the excuse of our project for another month. But I wanted to spend all the time in the world with her.

I wasn't going to tell her that yet though. She was dead set on Paris, and I didn't want to change her plans. I also didn't want to scare her off. But she, Iris Briggs, and I were endgame. And I wanted to ease her into the idea of that. "I'm sorry, Iris."

"It's okay. I'm not insecure or jealous. Okay, a little jealous, but I get it. Did she have plans with—what is that guy's name again? Charlie?"

"Yeah. So she's in the same boat as us."

"Charlie and I should form a support group."

"We probably could go out together if you wanted to."

"I think it's going to be a minute before Clara and I are, like, you know, *friends*-friends."

"Yeah, I get that. But I'm really sorry. I'll make this up to you tomorrow. Okay? That's just about enough time for my mother to get bored of me."

"Okay. Look, it's fine, honestly. I get it. I have some reading I want to catch up on. And there's a lot of stuff I need to do to edit the photos, picking out the best ones, seeing which ones work for the illustrated double exposure."

"I wanted to do that with you."

"We will. I'm just going to do the preliminary sifting. The dregs of the work. You'd hate that stuff. It's boring."

She had a point there. But still, I didn't want to make her do it all by herself. "Are you sure?"

"Oh my god, Keaton. It's fine. I'll see you tomorrow. Hell, if you're up tonight, call me. I might even sneak out of my room."

I clutched a hand to my chest as I gasped. "Oh my god, Iris Briggs, what have I done to you?"

"You have just encouraged my inner bad girl to come out and play."

"I am so here for that. Okay, I'll see you tomorrow. I love you," I said then hung up.

For a moment after I hung up, the words hung in the air, practically still echoing against the walls.

What.

The.

Fuck.

The words had just tumbled out of my mouth, unexpectedly. As if I had meant to say them all along. What was she thinking? What did I just do?

My mother sent a text.

Mom Monster: Do not be late.

Mom Monster: I'm serious.

Jesus Christ. I had to go. Excellent.

I'd deal with Iris and the three little words later.

Lunch was not nearly as terrible as I thought it would be. My mother was in a mellow mood. Actually, a pretty good one.

There was laughing, there was talking. Mom touched my arm and said she was proud of me—as she chattered about my grades and rugby season and how it was going to be amazing and how I not only had scouts looking at me, but from the UK and New Zealand teams. Which was true. But how did she know all of that?

She's a Constantine, I reminded myself. There was no way she wasn't keeping tabs on me here at school.

It was strange how I was almost warmed by it, even if it meant she'd delegated taking an interest in me to someone else. But it still showed she cared.

The Blairs seemed dutifully impressed, and then conversation segued off into the usual Bishop's Landing gossip and travel talk, which was always the same. Someone sleeping with someone else, so-and-so getting ready for their trip to the Seychelles, the Morellis are sniffing around some development opportunities on our side of the city, etc.

My mother was shockingly pleasant the entire time. Even her normally cool eyes were warm, and her smile —only rarely bestowed—was out in full force as she charmed the Blairs. As she charmed *me*.

This was the mother I had seen only glimpses of in the past five years, this was the mother I remembered from before Dad's death. This was what it felt like to be fully her son, someone who had value in the here and now, and not just as Winston's clone someday. Maybe...maybe I'd been too hard on her?

If she was making an effort now, then shouldn't I as well?

We took her car back to campus after lunch, and as I watched the red and gold trees flash by the window as the driver sped down the highway, my mother cleared her throat. I looked across to where she sat next to me, calmly studying her pale pink nails.

"How are you and Clara doing together? Have you thought any more about carrying this relationship into college? Beyond?"

All the happiness, all the light that I'd been feeling earlier began to dim. A bitter taste crawled up my throat. "That is not going to happen."

My mother pinned me with a cool look. "We need it to happen. The Blairs are thinking about expanding their portfolios with investments in WC Tech—but it's the kind of deal that only happens with an ironclad family tie in place, which is why we don't need any broken hearts complicating things."

"That's not what this is. I'm not breaking Clara's heart."

The look got even cooler. "Can't you see your family needs you? All I'm asking is that you try to make things last with Clara."

Clara. Right. That was the only reason she'd come. *For the Blairs and their money.* I was such a fucking idiot. I'd thought she'd come for me. For once. I thought she'd turned up for me.

"I don't love her," I said finally. "And she doesn't love me."

"Love is not the only thing that makes a marriage," my mother responded, pushing her fingertips against her temple as if she was getting a headache. "Take it from me. Your father and I—we had a strong partnership. A good partnership. And we did love each other. But when that love grew . . . complicated . . . what kept us together was the family and what the family needed. I've made sacrifices too—more than plenty—to make sure that there is a legacy for you and your brothers and sisters to carry on. Because that's what being a Constantine means; that's what it looks like to grow up and succeed in a world hell-bent on tearing you down."

I stared back at her. "I want to help, but I'm not Winston, Mom. I can't be blood on the family altar."

She wrinkled her nose. "Don't be dramatic. All I'm asking is for you to think about your father's legacy. What he died for—what he was killed for. We can't let that sacrifice go to waste."

By the time we parked in visitors' parking, I was in a hell of a mood.

I wanted to tell Mom everything about me and Clara and Charlie and Iris so then it would all be out in the open, and I could just be with the girl I loved. But I also wanted to make my mother proud and honor my father's legacy.

I wanted my own life.

But I also didn't want to fuck over my brothers and sisters.

I climbed out of the car and then helped Mom out, watching as she straightened her dress and smoothed her hair. The sun accentuated the tiny lines by her eyes and mouth, and caught the thin strands of silver threading through the blond, making them gleam.

She was still beautiful, Caroline Constantine, but it struck me then that she was getting older. That she might be tired from steering a family that walked a razor-thin line between prosperity and utter destruction. That she might truly and genuinely need my help —not because she was controlling or cold, but because the work of running the Constantine family was too big for one person alone.

"Do you remember how your father loved the sea?" Mom asked as we walked towards the stone stairs where Clara and her parents waited for us. Her voice was no longer cool, but wistful, and a little bit sad.

"Yeah."

"Every time he'd get to Bishop's Landing, it wouldn't matter how late it was or if we had guests waiting—he'd go right through that back door into the gardens and stare at the ocean. As if he wasn't really home until he saw it."

I remembered. It's why I'd sketched him that day, wanting to capture an image that was so indelible to my childhood. The image of Lane Constantine looking out onto the water, wind ruffling his hair, his shoulders and back relaxing as the business of the day or week melted from his body. He was no longer a billionaire, a mogul, and emperor ruling over an empire of both legal and less-than-legal realms, but a husband about to go kiss his wife on the cheek. He was a father about to hug all his children and ruffle their hair and ask about their day at school.

He was a man at home.

My throat closes at the memory; my eyes burn at the thought of him.

Fuck, I miss him.

My mother continued. "Your father loved the sea because it meant he was home. But that home won't be there for the next generation of Constantines unless we safeguard it. I know I can count on you." Her voice started to break when she added, "You're such an amazing son. He would have been so proud to see you now."

These words—words that I'd wanted to hear for years. My throat clenched even harder.

"Mom?"

"I love you, Keaton," she said, eyes shining. She blinked fast, swallowing it. "He loved you. Anything I've asked of you hasn't been about control . . . it's been about love."

"I—" I stared at her.

It had been so long since I could really remember feeling her love, so long since I'd felt the glow of being her son all for myself, instead of feeling jealous and resentful that my brothers and sisters soaked up all her attention.

I couldn't marry Clara. I couldn't even date her in college. But to keep pretending for now, until I could make my mom understand? Until Clara was ready to come clean about Charlie?

What could it hurt?

It will hurt Iris.

But my mother would be gone soon, and then Clara and I would resume our usual pattern of staying out of each other's way, and Iris and I could get back to us.

"I can keep trying with Clara for now."

She touched my shoulder. "Thank you, Keaton. This means the world."

Subconsciously, I glanced around for Iris, searching the crowds for her smile. Just seeing her smile would stop this ugly churn of doubt and flattered desperation inside me.

You told Iris you love her, and now you're agreeing to pretend to love someone else. You're really ready to see her right now?

Okay. No, not really.

And I knew she would be making herself scarce anyway. This was Parents' Weekend. Her parents would be busy playing host to all the visitors. And this time she wouldn't be needed to help, since most parents would be wanting to talk to the headmaster about grades and behavior—nothing she could help with or was even allowed to hear. She was all alone today.

But I was glad she wasn't around to see what I was going to do.

This is a bad idea. You don't want to do this.

No, I didn't. But neither could I relinquish the feeling of my mother's love and pride in me so easily.

But Iris. . .

But this was just for today . . . just for the year. Until Clara went to Duke with Charlie, until I got my first stage of trust fund money. Why shouldn't I get to enjoy this version of my mother for a while longer? Why shouldn't I get to feel what it was like to be Winston and always do the right thing?

When we approached Clara and her parents on the stairs, Clara gave me a smile. And her mother clapped her hands. "Let's get a picture of the happy couple together."

Automatically, my arms wrapped around Clara's waist, and I pulled her against me in a pose we had practiced a million times.

My gaze flickered up. For once I had Mom's approval. Her attention.

And that felt so very, very close to being cared about. Like she finally gave a shit that I was her son.

I turned and gave Clara a tight smile.

She frowned and lifted a dark brow. "You okay?"

"Yeah. I'm fine," I whispered. The fear and pride and the need to please my mom mixed together inside me, like a whirlpool of toxic chaos. All I'd ever wanted was to be a real part of this family, to prove I had value, and now I had my in. My chance.

With every muscle tense and every nerve thrumming like I was going into battle, I leaned in and kissed Clara. Not just a regular kiss. But the kind of kiss that left no argument about our relationship.

We always touched strategically at school. Holding hands, sitting in laps, even chaste brushes of lips when it was warranted. But I'd never kissed her like this. It was always just quick pecks before, but this—this was a real kiss. This was the kind of kiss I'd given Iris.

My lips molded over Clara's lips, the pressure posses-sive and claiming. Heat seared over the back of my neck and between my shoulder blades, stinging and hot, like I was being watched. Like I was being judged.

It was shame, maybe. Or guilt.

The cost of doing business with my mother.

I eased back, and Clara blinked. Slightly dazed, she lifted a brow but then her gaze skittered over to my mother and back to me, and she understood. She gave me a slight nod. And then ran a finger delicately under her bottom lip as if to fix her lipstick. That prickly heat feeling didn't stop. It was all too familiar.

Why was that?

And then I knew. My gaze searched the crowd. And I found her.

Iris.

Under the tree watching me.

I'd chosen my mom. My family. Over the girl I'd fallen for.

And now she knew.

*I*n the week since New York, in the stolen moments in the library and in his dormitory bedroom—and yes, the darkroom again—I hadn't dared hope. I wouldn't let myself.

It was much too ridiculous to fall in love with Keaton. It was even more ridiculous still to expect him to fall in love with me.

How many girls must he have screwed here at Pembroke? How many girls were still lining up to be screwed by him, by this ridiculously handsome idol of the school? I'd be a fool to take the moments we had together—urgent, sweet moments when he murmured the most wonderful filth in my ear—and turn them into some kind of romance.

But I *was* a fool.

Because between that first night in New York and now, I'd somehow done the unthinkably dumb thing, and I'd fallen in love with him.

And no amount of guarding my heart—no amount of reminding myself that *we're the real fucking deal* was just boy-speak for liking me and my body, and not some kind of code for love—could smother the daydreams and the fantasies. Him and me, hands laced as we walked through Paris. Him and me years from now, with rings and tuxes and a white dress—

No, I couldn't hope. And every time hope dared to sprout, like a tender green shoot of spring, I crushed it and buried it. And I'd keep crushing it and burying it until the end of time. I could do that. I was a smart girl. I had no interest in going to Paris with a broken heart.

But then—this morning on the phone—

I love you.

His words sank into my skin like hooks, they burned themselves onto the curves of my heart.

He loved me.

And for two glorious hours, I walked on air.

The Giant Oak was set on a small rise near the edge of the forest, and it was an excellent spot for making out due to its size and the deep hollow between two of its big roots. It was easy to nestle in there on the forest-facing side of the tree and out of sight of the school and kiss until the cold drove you back indoors.

It was also an excellent spot for surveying the grounds —the gentle rise that hosted the oak gave an excellent vantage over the lawn, quad, and buildings—and I sat there with my back against the trunk, watching parents and students mill around the buildings as small, stunned smiles chased themselves across my face.

He said he loved me.

I'd come to the oak because if I couldn't be with Keaton, then I needed to be somewhere that reminded me of him, as if running my fingers through the cool grass where we were supposed to be kissing right now would make up for the fact that we weren't touching at all, that he was currently with Clara instead of me.

I was jealous of that, of course, jealous of any time she got to spend with him, jealous that it was her that got to be part of the family—but the jealousy was soothed by the memory of his words.

I love you.

He loved me.

As if summoned by my thoughts alone, Keaton appeared, unfolding from a gleaming Bentley like the muscular king he was and then was joined by a slender blonde woman with a regal bearing that screamed *generational wealth*. Whatever she was saying to Keaton as they walked was upsetting, I surmised, because the set of Keaton's shoulders slumped and he was nodding his head at the ground, as if he was looking into his own grave.

As if he was remembering something painfully and indelibly sad.

I leaned forward as they talked, wishing I could be down there with Keaton, touching the place behind his ear like he liked me to do. I hated that his mother was making him feel this way; I hated that parents had this power over us. That they could take good days and turn them wretched just with a few words.

The minute Keaton was free, I would go to him and I would kiss him until he smiled again. I would kiss him until he murmured those sweet words to me, and I finally got to murmur them back.

I love you.

Together, Keaton and his mother arrived at the shallow stone stairs that led up to the cluster of brick and stone buildings making up the Pembroke campus. My stomach tightened when I realized people were waiting for them on the steps—Clara Blair and two adults who were presumably her parents.

What happened next felt like it happened in slow motion. Like time had frozen and each millisecond stretched to the length of a year.

Keaton's arms went around Clara in an affectionate embrace.

And after a beat, maybe two, he tilted his face down towards hers.

My fingers were numb. My lips were numb. Even my heart beat numbly.

No, I thought to myself. *No.*

His hand cupped the back of her head, her brunette hair spilling out below his grip in glossy waves, and then he brought his lips down to hers. It wasn't a pretend kiss. It wasn't a kiss meant to placate a parental audience. It was a kiss like he meant it. A kiss like he wanted her. A kiss that said *we're the real fucking deal.*

And it wasn't meant for me.

It couldn't have lasted more than a few seconds, but when Keaton finally broke away from Clara, I felt like I'd aged a year. Five years. I felt like I'd been standing there watching him kiss Clara for as long as the Giant Oak had been sitting there on its little hill.

And when Keaton's eyes—somehow, impossibly—lifted and found mine, I felt more than old.

I felt broken.

I turned and fled, my feet pounding over the grass as I ran all the way back to the headmaster's residence, and not once did I look back—not because I was afraid he'd be chasing me.

But because I knew he wasn't.

He'd lied.

That was the first real thought that pushed its way forward after god only knew how many minutes I spent sobbing into my bed.

He'd lied about everything. About him and Clara being pretend, about them not kissing, about all of it, and I'd been stupid enough to believe him. So desperate to hear what I wanted to hear that I refused to look the truth solidly in the eye and see what any idiot could have seen.

Keaton Constantine was using me. He was doing what guys like him had always done—he'd come, he'd fucked, he'd conquered, using any means necessary, and it was so *obvious* in retrospect, that I wanted to bang my head against the wall. How many times had I thought the king of the school couldn't possibly want the new girl? How many times had I marveled that this arrogant Adonis desired *me* of all people?

How many times since this morning alone had I giggled in wonder to myself that this muscle-carved idol might love me?

Why hadn't I listened to my gut?

Why hadn't I known that he would do what all idols invariably did, and fall?

He'd never loved me. He'd loved fucking me maybe, but that was the extent of it, and if I'd ever believed otherwise, well, I only had myself to blame.

I rolled over to my side, still crying. Tears soaked the duvet beneath my face, and my stomach was starting to hurt from all the heaving sobs. When would I stop crying? When would I stop seeing Keaton's hand in her hair, his mouth firm and dominating over hers?

In my jeans pocket, my phone buzzed against my bottom. Sniffling, I pulled it out to see Keaton's name on the screen.

No.

No.

I declined the call, and then put my phone on my end table.

It immediately buzzed again. And again. Followed by short buzzes—text messages. Text messages that I absolutely refused to read. I couldn't stand to listen to any more lies, any more excuses. He would tell me it meant nothing, that it was all for show, but I knew what I saw. I knew what a passionate kiss from him looked like.

And maybe I had been stupid. Maybe I had been the world's biggest idiot.

But I would break my own fingers before I let Keaton sweet-talk me back into stupidity again.

I turned off my phone.

In the silence that followed, my tears returned in full force. I stared across the room at the sweater dress flung over my desk chair—the same one I'd dry-fucked Keaton while wearing—and I stared at my camera, which had had Keaton's strong fingers curled around it in New York.

I flopped to my back so I didn't have to see all the reminders of him. And suddenly, I felt so *lonely*, so utterly and miserably bereft that I couldn't stand it any longer.

I couldn't just cry in my bed all day, reliving that horrible kiss with its horrible implications; I needed to leave, I needed to do something, see somebody—

It hit me nearly as hard as seeing the kiss had.

I needed to see my friends.

I needed to cry in Sera's bed while she and Aurora promised to hold him down while Sloane skinned him alive. I needed ice cream and trashy TV and a fresh, dry pillow to wet with my tears.

Without wasting a single second, I threw my laptop and phone into my bag—so that if my dad stopped by my room, he'd assume I went somewhere to study—and I made my way to the girls' dorms, sniffling the entire way.

*S*alty tears tracked down my face. No matter how hard I wished, they wouldn't stop. The well of emotion had come rolling through me, crashing through me like someone who'd stood a little too close to shore, and unfortunately as I tried to stand back up, another wave came to knock me down and choked me, sending salt water up my nose.

Serafina rubbed my back. "Jesus, Iris, I'm so sorry. He is such a dick cunt."

"What the fuck is a dick cunt?" Aurora asked, brows furrowed.

Sera shrugged. "I don't know. It sounds bad though."

Sloane pursed her lips. "I know a thing called a Colombian necktie; you want me to do it to him?"

I lifted my gaze to hers. "What the hell is a Colombian necktie?"

She shrugged. "Well, first I'd slit his throat, right? And then, you pull his tongue out through it. Sounds fitting for a lying cheat bag."

I could only blink at Sloane. "What in the world?"

Aurora shook her head. "No, no, no, no. That's too on the nose. We have to make him pay slowly, over a period of time. Make him rue the day. We need to make every single thing about his existence hurt. Make it excruciating."

I stared at her. Her unusual golden eyes flickered with glee and merriment.

"Jesus Christ, you're crazy, do you know that? Actually, you know what?" I pointed at both her and Sloane. "Both of you are batshit. We're not necktying anyone. And I'm not here for the revenge, but what I will tell you is I'm going to stop fucking crying. My mistake was in thinking that I wasn't the cool girl, that I was the lucky one. But no—*he* was the lucky one."

Sera gave me a brisk nod. "Hell yes. *He* is the lucky one in this scenario and *he* fucked up. You are not going to sit here and cry for him. You are a badass. You're Iris

Briggs. Your whole future is ahead of you. You're going to be this huge photographer one day, and he's going to beg to come to your exhibits. And all of us will be there, and we will laugh as he is turned away at the door."

I did like the sound of that. "Keep talking."

Sera and the others grinned. Aurora handed me a glass with a dubious-colored mixture inside it. "What's this?"

She grinned. "Well, I won't say where I learned the skill—" her eyes slid over to Sloane "—but I happen to be a decent lock picker. I broke into Keaton's room and stole his expensive bottle of rum. It's a fifteen-hundred-dollar bottle, so you're going to drink it."

My mouth hung open. Not that she'd broken into his room, or stolen his bottle of rum, but the fact that it cost fifteen hundred dollars, Jesus. "I don't—I don't really drink."

"Well, we will drink in your honor this very expensive rum, but also, you're going to have one. He popped your cherry and fucked you over. You can't just let it go without finishing his rum."

A flush crept up my neck, and Sera blinked at me.

"*Wow*," Aurora said, stunned. "I was just guessing, but *really*? You had sex with him?"

"Iris, you didn't!" Sera exclaimed before I could answer. "And you didn't tell me?"

I swallowed. "I did. But I didn't want to tell you, because I knew I was being an idiot over him."

I was that clichéd girl who believed that the gorgeous, rich golden boy could have fallen in love with her, that we were more alike than we were *different*. That he understood me, and that he wanted my dreams for me as much as I did. But I had been duped. That wasn't on Keaton. That was on me.

Aurora gave me a sympathetic look. "You wouldn't be the first one."

"Jesus Christ." Sera rubbed my back. "Okay firstly, I'm never forgiving you for not telling me immediately. Secondly, who you sleep with is your business—well, also mine, but mostly yours. No one gets to judge you for who you take to bed. You are a modern-times girl. You can sleep with whomever you want, whenever you want. Hell, you can still give him a repeat revenge bone. That's up to you. No one gets to judge you for that, least of all yourself. You slept with him because you are Iris Briggs and you wanted to. Don't beat yourself up for it."

"I know. It's just . . . it was my first time, and it was a textbook first time, you know?"

Sloane coughed a laugh. "You mean awkward fumbling?"

I shook my head. "No, it was that perfect kind of thing. He wasn't at all awkward. He was gentle. But there was also something that said he couldn't hold back. A feeling that told me I made him lose control. He hadn't wanted to hurt me. And it had been amazing. You know, beautiful and perfect, and you get to have an orgasm for the first time kind of thing."

Aurora lifted a brow. "Really? The first time?"

"Yeah." I glanced around. "Is that normal?"

Sera shrugged. "I don't know what normal is, but look, take the experience for what it was. An experience. Even if it was with Keaton Constantine. It was positive, and that's what you needed at the time. Now, is that going to preclude us from kicking his ass? *Hell no.* There are still months left of school, and we can make his life a living hell until then."

I shook my head. "As much fun as Colombian neckties and a slow steady plan of revenge sound, my best revenge is getting the fuck out of Dodge. I don't need to be here. In fact . . ." I reached over to my bag and pulled out my laptop, pulling up the webpage I visited nightly like it was some kind of virtual shrine.

Aurora leaned over and looked, a shot glass of amber rum balanced easily in her hand. "Your Sorbonne thing," she said, understanding.

"What Sorbonne thing?" Sera demanded.

"She wants to go to this pre-degree program in Paris," Aurora explained for me. "She's got the credits to get her diploma now if she wants, so she could go."

"They provide housing and a student stipend too," I said quietly. "Because my college fund is strictly for a degree-seeking program, it's the only way I can go without asking for my father's money. Which he'd never give me."

"So you want to leave here," Sera said, sounding unimpressed.

I looked up at her, suddenly feeling like I'd like that rum very much right now.

"I can't stay here. Not with him."

Sloane and Aurora seemed to agree with me. But Sera pressed her lips together. She did "disdainful mother" very well. "I don't know, Iris. Look, I'm here for you. And I just think Keaton deserves to pay. He really does. But do I think you should run? No. I think he needs to face what he did. I think he owes you an apology. Now, either he does that voluntarily or we make him give you one, but something needs to happen."

I shook my head. "Nope. I just want out. I want to be gone from here. Dad's moved schools almost every two years, you know? And after Isabelle left, I think they needed a change—their entire lives had revolved around her and once she was gone, the place we were at didn't feel like home anymore. So we came here for them, but no one consulted me on how I felt, what I needed. So this time, I'm going to do what I need to do for *me*. I want to go."

Sera winced. "That sucks. Just when you're getting settled."

"Tell me about it. But you three can visit me in Paris anytime. You should come."

Sera bit her nail delicately. "Look, it's not like you're going to make any changes right now. You still have to, at least, see if you're accepted. Not to mention telling your parents, convincing your father to let you graduate early, and booking your trip."

I did need to make some kind of plan. I couldn't just up and get on the plane tomorrow. I had to wait, be patient. Who knew how much longer until I heard if I was accepted? "Okay, you have a point. I need a better plan than *fuck this shit, I'm leaving.*"

She snorted a laugh. "Yes, *you* definitely need a *plan.*"

I looked at my nails. "I'm not that bad, am I?"

My friends nodded. "Um, yeah, you're very much a planner. We dig it though. Team Iris all the way."

The four of us picked up our shot glasses, clinked them, and tossed them back. I coughed at the burn at the back of my throat. Jesus fucking Christ. But the liquid did go down smooth after the initial shock of it. And it warmed everything on the way down.

The other three didn't even seem to notice. Sera peered at her glass. "Ooh, that's nice. I never thought I could rob Keaton blind with a rum drink. I thought he was one of those pompous assholes who swirls their scotch like they were important. But he has taste. And a rum, no less. If he wasn't such a douche asshole, I might like him."

Aurora peered at her glass too. "You know what, fuck this, let me find a chaser."

She walked over to Sera's mini fridge, yanked it open, and saw a bottle of Pom juice. She got a pitcher on top of the fridge and then poured some of the Pom juice she found into it, added the rum, swirled it around, and then poured little shots of it. That went down much smoother. A little too smooth, if you ask me.

As we were on our third shots, I glanced around the room at the girls sitting around me. I hadn't thought this year would yield anything normal. But despite Keaton lying to me, using me, and breaking my heart, completely degrading it, I'd made some good friends here. The kind of friends that I probably needed in my life. Ones that wouldn't let me get away with being boring old Iris. Ones that pushed me to be different, to try different things, to experience life.

I smiled at them. "So who's going to join me in Paris next summer?"

All three of them raised their glasses, downed them, then slammed the glasses back down onto Sera's dark wood coffee table. Sera clapped. "Me, for sure. Whether you decide to go now, or you leave at the end of June, best know that come July, I will be with you. And there will be shopping to be had."

I grinned. "All that Parisian shopping will need a bigger, fancier place. You realize I'm going to live in a shoebox, right?"

She scoffed. "No, no, no. When I come visit, we're going to rent a giant fucking Airbnb, and it's going to be fabulous. Then we're going to get rid of all the boring things that you took with you because you were being frugal about money. We're going to sell all those things and buy something fun and exciting."

"Hear, hear," Sloane said.

"I second that. Actually, make that 'third that.'"

I laughed. "Guys, shopping isn't really my thing."

Sera bumped her shoulder into mine. "That's because you've never done it right. Now, if you did wait, I would just come with you. I'd go see my mom for plans, and we'd set up a place and meet cute French boys."

Aurora butted in. "Oh, you are not doing that without me."

"Me neither. We're here for that."

I laughed. "But Sera, you guys—what about your parents?"

Sera waved her hand. "If I come see you and wait around for two weeks, then I join them in St. Kitts, it's the same thing. They go for a month every year. I was going to go with them for two weeks and then I'd come and see you. No big deal. I'll just pop in."

"Either way, you're coming to Paris?"

"You better believe it."

"Who needs Keaton Constantine anyway, right?"

She nodded. "Absolutely. Because remember, you are the hot girl, and he is a pencil-dick-ass face."

I bit my bottom lip, my body clenching as I remembered his dick. "Yeah, except it wasn't exactly a pencil dick."

All three of them stared at me. But then Sera howled. "Oh my god, you have been withholding. Tell us *everything*."

I snorted a laugh. Even though my belly knotted, a little girl talk was what the doctor ordered.

A little girl talk was healing. It didn't matter that I'd fallen for Keaton's bullshit. It didn't matter that he'd broken my heart. What mattered was, I didn't need him. What mattered was, I was strong all on my own.

As Sera and the others said, *I* was the *it* girl. He was just someone who'd been lucky enough to bask in my presence for a short time, not the other way around.

As far as I was concerned, Keaton Constantine didn't exist.

And right as I decided that, I heard a chime from my still-open laptop.

An email.

Curious, I woke up the screen and looked—and then promptly forgot how to breathe.

It was from the program coordinator at the Sorbonne.

I've been accepted to the pre-degree program.

I still couldn't breathe.

The director also wanted me to know that starting this week, all the program students would have access to the student housing near the campus, in order to give them plenty of time to get adjusted to the city before the seminars and work started in earnest.

I stared at the screen for a long time, wondering if the rum had gotten to me. But no—this wasn't the rum. This was real life.

And I was in.

I was going to Paris.

I was a colossal fuckup.

I could hear Clara behind me as I tore away from her and stalked up the stairs. "Keaton, what are you doing? *Keaton?*"

I wanted to run after Iris. But she was gone, and anyway, what would I say if I caught her? *It's exactly what it looked like? Don't worry, baby, I thought about my mom the entire time?*

Jesus Christ. It sounded pathetic and creepy even in my head.

Clara caught up to me, touching my elbow. "Hey, what's wrong with you? That kiss, what was that for?"

I ran my hands through my hair. My gut churned, and I felt like I was going to vomit.

I felt ill.

You are a colossal fuckup.

"I'm sorry. I shouldn't have kissed you."

She crossed her arms over her chest. "Yeah, clearly. But that's not what I'm talking about. Why did you kiss me in front of *everyone* else? What's gotten into you?"

I mean, what the hell was I supposed to say? "You know the deal. I was faking it for the cameras, basically."

Her sigh said it all. She was exhausted. Just like I was. Tired of the lies. Tired of the bullshit. "We've been faking it for so long. Some of it is automatic . . . but that was not an automatic kiss. We have never put on that good of a show."

I couldn't breathe. It almost felt like I was going to pass out. Back and forth, back and forth, I paced.

"Fuck. Fuck. Fuck."

Clara put up her hands and approached me warily like you would a wounded animal. "Okay. Okay, calm down. Relax. What's going on?"

"My mother, she said she needed me, she wanted me to make our relationship look good. She wants your father to invest in Winston's new company eventually and—"

I couldn't fucking breathe. The words wouldn't come out. I had hurt Iris to please my mother. Iris—the one person who had always been there for me. The one person who told me the truth, the person I would rather see smile than anything else. I had hurt her deliberately. I was the worst kind of human being.

Clara's voice went low. "Okay. Okay, relax. This has gone on too long."

I frowned at her. "What?"

"*This. You. Me.* It's gone on too long. It served a purpose for a while, but it doesn't serve that purpose anymore. I'm going to tell my parents that we're done. And I'm going to tell them it's my fault. And that I have a boyfriend who does not have a penny to his name, but a scholarship to Duke, and I want to be with him."

My jaw unhinged. "Why would you do that?"

"Well, for starters, so none of this blows back on you and your family, since they do, in fact, want my parents for something."

"I've never really known you to be altruistic, Clara."

She shrugged. "I'm sick of it—the lies. And I can see the way you look at her. I might not like Little Miss Perfect, but I do like you. You're like family. And if I can help, I will." She turned to leave, but my mother rounded the corner and found us just in time.

"Keaton, what is going on?"

Clara's parents came around too. *Oh, fantastic.* Everyone was here to witness the show.

Clara cleared her throat. "Mom, Dad, listen, there's something you need to know. Keaton and I aren't—" She faltered, as if suddenly realizing the storm she was about to cause.

She looked at me with wide eyes, and I picked up where she left off, touching my hand to her elbow to let her know she had my support. "Actually, Mr. and Mrs. Blair, the truth is, Clara and I haven't been truly dating for a long time."

My mother's hand went to her throat, but she didn't speak.

Clara, however, was not going to let me go down alone. She patted her mother on the arm. "Mom, what Keaton is trying to say is, we were thrown together so often, and the expectation seemed to be that we were going to be together. So we pretended we were. And since both of you were quite happy, it gave us some freedom to do what we wanted on our own. You never seemed to question anything I did if I said I was with Keaton."

The furrowed brow and lines around my mother's mouth said it all. She turned to Clara's parents with an apologetic smile. "I think this is some kind of misunderstanding. Young people these days, their relationships always go up and down, you know how it is."

She kept talking, but Clara's words were the only ones her parents were listening to. "Look, I thought you wouldn't approve," she was saying, "but I have an actual boyfriend. And he doesn't have a dime to his name."

It was her mother's turn to touch her pearls in shock. "Clara, what are you saying?"

"What I'm saying is that I'm completely in love with someone else. His name is Charlie Jones. A completely common name for a completely common guy. Except to me, he's not common at all. He's extraordinary. And he treats me exactly how I should be treated. I love him. And he loves me. I'm not going to Harvard next year. I'm going to Duke."

Her father raised a hand. "Now, wait just a minute young lady, you are not—"

She shook her head. "We *lied*, Dad. Don't you see? It was never real, and it can never be real because we're both in love with different people. Keaton too."

The parents all swiveled their heads to me in tandem.

"It's true, I'm in love with someone else," I admitted. "Her name is Iris Briggs. Her father is the headmaster. I really care about her, and I want to be with her. I'm not going to fake this anymore."

Clara's father and mother looked back to their daughter. Her mother whispered softly, "So you've been *pretending* to date Keaton?"

"Yeah. Sorry."

Her mother shook her head. "But why?"

"Because I knew you wouldn't approve of Charlie."

Her mother pursed her lips. "Clara Blair, I'll have you know that despite your father's fancy old-money name, he was penniless when I married him. And I didn't give a fuck back then. I'm horrified you thought we would be like that."

Clara opened her mouth then closed it again, and then tried one more time to get words out, but to no avail. Her father shook his head. "Your mother is right. I had been living on the generosity of family and scholarships, but her parents accepted me without any conditions. There is no reason for us to not like anyone you date. Especially if they're actually a good person. We'd like to meet your actual boyfriend—Charlie. Not that Keaton isn't a fine boy. But if you don't love each other, what's the point?"

My mother made one last attempt to salvage this. "Listen, they're young, they're impulsive . . . maybe we should talk about—"

Mr. Blair shook his head. "Caro, if the kids don't want to date, what's the purpose?"

My mother pinked, but when she spoke, she had steel in her voice. "And who is this Iris Briggs girl?"

"I told you, she's the headmaster's daughter."

Clara's father frowned. "Yes, I met her. Smart girl."

I grinned at that. "Yeah, she is."

I could tell that just the fact that Clara's parents even knew of Iris upped her status in my mother's eyes immediately. "Yes, you know, Keaton, I'd love to meet her."

I couldn't be sure if she was saying that to save face or not. I decided to take it as a genuine offer. "I'd like that too . . . but I have to be able to trust that you can accept her for who she is, and not condemn her for who she isn't. I love you, Mom, but I can't be what you need anymore, and I won't make Iris be either. I'm done. And I need to go and find her and tell her exactly that."

Clara stepped up to me and gave me a big hug. "I'm not in love with you, but I do love you very much." She planted a kiss on my cheek and then gently let me go. "Go get your girlfriend back."

The heat spread through me at the uncomfortable emotional display. "Thanks, Clara."

"Anytime."

I left them all behind to find my girlfriend.

That is if she is, in fact, still your girlfriend.

One problem at a time.

~

She wasn't answering my calls. She wasn't answering my texts.

After checking the Giant Oak to make sure she hadn't doubled back, I swung by my room, even though I knew the chances of her waiting for me there were extremely slim.

That only left one place—her house—and I didn't want to crash in unannounced, so I'd tried calling and texting, but to no avail. I debated waiting, waiting until she responded . . . but what if she never responded? What if she never gave me a chance to apologize and make it right?

What if I've really lost her forever?

Panic choked me, and I knew I had to see her, I had to see those sweet blue eyes and hold her warm, slender hand while I told her everything, while I explained to her that Clara and I were done and I'd never hurt Iris like that again—*ever*.

When I reached the headmaster's residence, I was panting and out of breath. My hands were shaking, not from exhaustion, but from worry. I banged at the door, but nobody answered.

God, she could be anywhere. I banged again. "Iris. Please God, Iris, open the door."

When the door did open, it wasn't Iris, it was her mother. "Oh, Mrs. Briggs, I'm so sorry to disturb you. I didn't mean to barge in, but I'm looking for Iris. I need to talk to her. There was a complete misunderstanding and—" I dragged in my breath, trying to calm myself down. "I'm so sorry. I, um, if I can only talk to her, if you can tell me where she is, I would really appreciate it."

Mrs. Briggs didn't seem *un*sympathetic to my desperation, but neither did she move out of the doorway to let me in. "I'm afraid Iris isn't in. She's gone to visit her friends in the dormitory."

Shit.

I knew my chances of getting Iris back probably diminished with every minute she spent with Sera and them. They weren't exactly the biggest fans of the Hellfire Club—or me.

"Do you know when she'll be back?" I asked, past caring how reckless and despondent I sounded.

Iris's mother gave me a kind look. "I'm not sure when, but I will certainly tell her you stopped by . . .?"

And I realized that Iris's mother didn't even know my name. Because I'd never introduced myself—I'd never even tried. Because instead of being the kind of boyfriend that met his girlfriend's mom, I'd been the kind to make her hide while he pretended to date someone else.

Jesus, no wonder she wasn't answering my calls or texts. No wonder she wanted nothing to do with me.

"Thank you, Mrs. Briggs," I said, trying to keep my voice steady. "I'd appreciate that." And then I turned and left.

As much as I wanted to go to the girls' dormitory and haul Iris back to my room like a caveman, I knew there was no way I'd get past Sera or Aurora—or God help me, Sloane, who seemed like the kind of person who knew how to kill a man as painfully as possible.

So waiting it was, three impatient hours of it, checking my phone obsessively and drinking straight from a bottle of gin since I couldn't find my good rum. When enough time had passed that I thought I could reasonably go back to the headmaster's residence to check if she was home, I left my dorm and stepped out into the path that led to the headmaster's house.

Where I slammed straight into Serafina. "Jesus fucking Christ."

When I saw who it was, I righted myself and then helped her up. "Were you with Iris? Do you know where she is now?"

Serafina pursed her lips, and then narrowed her gaze to slits. Her eyes slid over me with nothing but venom. "You mean that poor girl that you humiliated in front of the whole school? She's around here somewhere, wishing to god that she had never met you."

I swallowed hard. "I fucked up. I know that."

"Do you? Because I'm pretty sure *guys like you* think the world owes you something. You thought that you didn't have to play by the rules, and you hurt her. But she deserved better than that."

"I know. I know I fucked up. And I need to fix it. Tell me, where can I find her?"

She shrugged. "I'm not sure. She was with us, but then she left, maybe to find her parents or something. I really don't know."

"I'm not a complete douchebag, Serafina."

"Then how about you prove it? Show me, don't tell me. Better yet, show Iris."

"You're right," I said, and Sera squinted up at me from behind her big, trendy glasses.

"Are you fucking with me right now, Constantine?" she demanded.

"No, I—" I sighed down at the tiny van Doren heiress. "I need to show her I'll never hurt her again, and I plan to. I will."

Something in my voice must have softened her, because she let out a sigh of her own. "You won't be able to see her tonight anyway. She's packing."

I thought I was done feeling panic; I thought there was no way I could feel any more misery. I was wrong.

"Packing?" I repeated hoarsely.

Sera gave me a look that was one part sympathy to three parts loyal friend. "I don't know if I should tell you . . ."

"Please," I croaked. "I have to know. Is she leaving Pembroke? For a while? For good? If she's leaving, I don't know what I'll do—I *love* her, Sera. I love her so much that it feels like I can't breathe sometimes. And if she's gone . . ."

The heiress considered me. "I've never seen you like this," she said.

"Like what?"

"Like a wreck. A messy, dumb wreck." Her mouth twisted to the side as she thought for a moment, and then she let out another sigh. "Iris was accepted to a pre-degree program at the Sorbonne. It starts next month, but the student housing is opening up this week. Which means she's leaving. Very soon."

My brain fizzed and popped, filling with static. None of this made sense. "But she can't leave tomorrow. She has classes. We have a project. She can't go anywhere until she graduates. She can't just *leave!*"

"She can," Sera said, a bit archly. "And she is. She's got more than enough credits to graduate early, and she talked with her dad about it after she got the acceptance email. They fought about it, but she threatened to go over his head to the board if he didn't let her go. She just texted to say he agreed to arrange her academic exit, and she'll be leaving for Paris tomorrow."

I cursed under my breath. Jesus Christ. I really fucked this up. "Tomorrow."

Sera's archness disappeared, and she gave me an understanding look. "Look, Iris has always known that she wanted something different, and she's been hoping for this Sorbonne thing since before she met you. This would have happened whether or not you broke her heart."

Knowing Serafina was right didn't make me feel any better. There was a difference between Iris chasing her dreams and Iris being chased away *to* her dreams because I'd hurt her.

"I can't let her leave like this," I said, staring up at the sky. It was early evening now, a perfect autumn twilight, cool and vibrant. I wished it were storming or gray, something to reflect my miserable mood. "If she leaves with the way things are . . . then it's over for us. Really over."

"I don't disagree," Sera said, not sounding like she cared very much. But then she added, "I guess . . . I guess, if I found out when her flight left, I could let you know. And you could show up at the airport and see if she'll talk to you there."

I had to resist the urge to pick her up and swing her around. "Really?"

She held up a finger. "On one condition. You stop going full stalker tonight, and let her enjoy this last night with her parents, okay? She deserves to say all the goodbyes she wants without you knocking down her door and blowing up her phone. If you can manage that, then I'll call you tomorrow morning with her flight info."

I did pick her up and swing her around that time. I couldn't help it, and surprisingly, she had a smile on her lips when I put her down.

"I'm still not rooting for you," she said, but the smile remained.

"That's okay," I told her. "I don't think I deserve to root for myself at this point."

he next morning, I was sitting in my parked car and trying not to scream with impatience when Serafina finally called.

"Which airport did she go to?" I asked, already starting the car and moving out of the lot.

"You're lucky I'm doing this," she said. "You don't deserve it."

There was a time when I would have argued with her. When I would have thought I deserved anything I wanted. No longer.

"You're right," I said. "I don't." There was no traffic up here—there never was—and I pushed the accelerator down to the floor as I sped down the narrow highway through the trees. "Please don't play coy with me, van Doren. I can't take it today. Where's she flying out of?"

"Firstly, Keaton Constantine," Serafina said, "I am never fucking *coy*. Secondly, I don't particularly care what you can or cannot take today, especially since you were the one who royally screwed up your chances with Iris to begin with."

I had nothing left to lose, and surprisingly, it barely bothered me at all to be brutally, humiliatingly honest. "If you tell me where she went, I'm going to grovel until she either forgives me or airport security drags me away."

Even from the other end of the call, I could tell Serafina liked that visual very much. "She does deserve a good grovel," she mused. "And the additional vengeance of watching you yanked off to a room for a body cavity search. Hmm."

I was getting close to the interstate now—I needed to know which way to go. "Sera."

"*Fine*," Serafina sighed. "She's flying out of Burlington. And you should hurry if you want to catch her before liftoff." She also gave me the airline, and when it was supposed to depart.

"Thanks, van Doren."

"You better grovel harder than fucking Darcy—"

I'd already thrown the phone on the passenger seat and sped up the car before she finished talking.

At first, it looked like no one was getting a Darcy-level grovel. When I got to the airport, it was to the knowledge that Iris's plane had just finished boarding, and she was about to be in the fucking air and lost to me.

But I didn't grind Croft Wells into the rugby field every season because I gave up easy. I stalked up to the airline desk, pulled out my wallet, and played to win.

Which I did.

Twice.

Firstly, I was able to catch a connecting flight to JFK, even though it was leaving in less than an hour, which would get me to JFK in plenty of time for Iris's transatlantic flight.

Secondly, I was able to buy out the entire first class section of the flight from New York to Paris, and I upgraded Iris's seat. It took an obscene amount of money—thank God for my insane allowance—an even obscener amount of scowling, demanding, and coldly threatening since it involved rescheduling several other passengers, but I've found there's very little that stands in the way of a guy's will when enough money is lubricating the way.

And just like with sex, I made sure there was plenty of lubrication.

The flight to JFK was short and uneventful, but I was still a mess the entire time. What would I say? What *could* I say? I hadn't just broken her heart—I'd broken her heart enough to send her running across the ocean without so much as a goodbye. That wasn't something I could fix with a simple apology. It wasn't even something I could fix with a grovel alone.

I was going to have to show her that I would put her first. Starting right now.

I waited to board the plane until the very last. Partly because I needed time to bribe a few flight attendants, and partly because I didn't want her to see me and then bolt. To that end, I lingered in the first-class bar until we were ready to push back from the gate, not wanting her to see me until it was too late.

Yes, it was a bastard move to wait until the doors were almost sealed to board the flight and finally take my seat, but what could I say? I was playing to win, after all.

When I finally stepped into the first-class cabin and saw her, I felt like I'd been tackled right down to the grass. The air left my body, my muscles flared—sparks and heat sizzled along every nerve.

She was fucking perfect. A vision of red hair and sweet features, long limbs folded in a graceful symmetry as she tucked her knees to her chest.

But it was her sadness that hit me like a fullback slamming me to the cold, wet ground. It was the drawn look to her face, the paleness behind those cinnamon-colored freckles. The red rims around her bright blue eyes.

I'd done that.

I'd done it by being selfish, by choosing the status quo. By choosing a family that wanted me only for how I could be of service over the girl who was willing to risk her heart and her pride just to be in my arms.

How could I have been so stupid?

I waited as a flight attendant brought a fizzing flute of champagne to her, presented on a silver platter. Iris took it wordlessly—and then froze when she saw what was under the flute.

A giant glossy picture of the sun over the New York skyline, breaking free from the clouds. The one she'd taken during our perfect weekend together.

Slowly, hesitantly, she picked it up and stared at it. And then her eyes gradually lifted, and she saw me standing at the far end of the aisle.

"Iris," I said softly, stepping forward as the flight attendant took her obvious cue and left.

Iris shook her head, her grip tightening on the picture. "What is this, Keaton? Why are you here?"

I reached Iris's seat and knelt down on both knees so I could look up into her beautiful face. "That is a reminder of how brilliant you are. Of how much you deserve to follow your dreams in Paris. And I'm here to tell you that I'm sorry. I know *sorry* is a word that doesn't mean much, and I know it especially doesn't mean much coming from me, but you still deserve to hear it."

With a shaking hand, she put her champagne flute on the small table next to her seat. She didn't meet my gaze. "Are you sorry you kissed her? Or only sorry that I saw it?"

"I'm sorry I kissed her. I'm sorry that I pretended to date her at all instead of deciding to come clean to my mom. I'm sorry that I chose her approval over your happiness. I thought all I wanted in the world was for her to be proud of me, but I was wrong, Iris, so wrong. If I'm not by your side, then nothing else matters."

She finally looked at me again, doubt pooling in her eyes. "That kiss—it wasn't a kiss born of duty. You kissed her like you kiss me. Like you meant it."

I knew I was supposed to be contrite, but the idea of wanting Clara made me snort. "I've never wanted her, Iris. I wanted more than anything to prove to my mother that I could help, and that I was part of the family, and that's why I kissed her the way I did. Not because I want her or because I'm in love with her, but because I was desperate to show my mom I could be a team player."

The flight attendant came by as the announcement came over the PA: it was time to sit down and buckle up. I sat in the seat across the aisle from Iris, hating the distance between us. I reached for her hand.

"It wasn't about Clara. It wasn't even about you. It was about me being too chickenshit to own that I want my own path. I want *you*, even if that means finally accepting that my family may never want me."

She took my hand and allowed me to wind my fingers through hers. She studied them with a small frown on her lips. "Does this have something to do with the dad you won't talk about?"

I shouldn't have been surprised that she remembered our conversation in the photography lab. But it was still like a small, icy arrow to the gut to hear it spoken out loud.

My family's pain. *My* pain.

"Yeah," I finally said, feeling that icy arrow burrow deeper. "His name was Lane."

Iris looked up to me, her expression transforming into one of sad horror. "Was?"

I took a deep breath. I had no practice talking about this; hell, even my mother barely talked about this with me. Nothing beyond the occasional muttered invective against the Morellis, or the slightly more common: *If he were still here . . .*

"He died five years ago. Murdered, we think, although no one ever got locked up for it. He was . . ." How could I even explain it? How could I even make it make sense? "He was the perfect patriarch, you know? Never flinched at what he had to do to keep the Constantine name and legacy as one that commanded respect. And then Winston stepped right up after his death, no questions asked, no hesitation. He was the perfect son, and I could never be as perfect as him, no matter how hard I tried. And I tried so hard, Iris. The grades, the rugby, the right friends . . ."

"And Clara," Iris supplied softly, her eyes searching mine.

"Yes. And Clara." I heaved a breath, knowing how it sounded. "This all seems so stupid when I say it out loud. Like something I should say to a therapist or some shit."

She squeezed my hand, and my heart lifted a little, buoyed with the slightest wave of hope. Beneath our feet, the plane vibrated and hummed with impending liftoff.

"You're wrong," Iris said. "I mean, not about the therapist—you should probably definitely go talk to one sometime about your dad and your family—but about it sounding stupid." She made a rueful face. "I completely understand about Winston. Isabelle has been the standard my parents have held me to my entire life. She's the perfect daughter. And all I ever wanted was for someone to see me exactly how I am . . ."

She looked down at the photograph in her lap.

". . . to see me for *who* I am," she finished quietly.

"I see you, Iris. I'm only sorry that I didn't see how much I needed you before it was too late."

We were in the sky now, soaring high above the same skyline that gleamed up from the picture in her lap.

She pulled her hand free, staring out her window. "I don't know . . ."

Another arrow lodged in me—this time in my chest. But I had expected this. "You don't have to know right now, baby. But I thought maybe—just maybe—you could give me the chance to show you how much I see you. How much I love you."

"In Paris?" Her brow furrowed. "But you'll have to go back the minute you land. School—"

"I can miss a few days."

"But your grades! And the project—"

"Fuck the project."

"But—rugby—"

"Is not as important as you. Not as important as you pursuing your passions and me helping you do everything you want. And it's only a practice or two. Everything will be fine."

Now that we were safely in the air, I got out of my seat and knelt by hers again.

"Please, Iris. You don't have to decide to take me back now. In fact, you can tell me to fuck off at any point. But let me show you how much I love you. Let me stay with you in Paris for a while. Let me join you there after graduation so we can be together for good."

She drew in a long breath. When it came out, it was shivery and hesitant. "I'm scared," she whispered. "I want you more than anything, and I love you—"

Hearing her say it was like swallowing pure sunshine. I was up and had her in my arms and then sat back down with her in my lap before she could say another word.

"You love me?" I asked, pulling a ponytail holder from the end of her long, messy braid and freeing her hair. "Because I love you, Iris. So fucking much. And I think I have since the first day of school."

She pulled her plump lower lip between her teeth. "Really?"

"Really."

"I'm scared, Keaton. I'm so scared. What if you hurt me again?"

I held her tight to my chest. "I will never hurt you again," I swore fiercely. "I promise, Iris. You're it for me. You're *it*. There's nothing else."

She tilted her face up to mine. "Nothing else?"

"And no one else. There's only you."

"Then I guess, maybe . . ." She paused, chewing on her lip again.

I felt like it was my heart between her teeth instead of her lip while I waited for her answer, but I waited patiently. It had to be her choice. Her forgiveness.

"Then I guess we can try," she finally said in a soft voice. "I'll try with you, Keaton. Try loving you and letting you love me."

"Thank fucking God," I said, letting out a ragged breath of existential relief. And I couldn't help it then —I had to kiss her. I yanked her even closer and sealed my mouth over hers.

She came alive in my arms, like Sleeping Beauty after her kiss. She dug her fingers into my hair and kissed me back, rubbing her sweet little ass over my lap as she did.

"It's a good thing there's no one else in first class right now," she breathed.

"I made sure of that."

I also made sure the flight attendants wouldn't come up to our cabin unless we called.

"You bought out first class just so you could do this?" Iris asked against my mouth.

With one hand, I grabbed the soft, folded blanket for her seat and wrapped it around her waist, and with my other, I sought out the sweet, secret place between her thighs. Within seconds, I had her panties pushed to the side and had her riding my fingers like a champ.

"No," I answered her. "I bought out first class so I could do *this*."

And then there were no more questions at all, just kisses and hot, sweet pleasure as we flew over the dark ocean on our way to the start of Iris's new life.

Our new life.

That summer . . .

*O*h my god. Sunlight streamed into my student apartment, turning everything in my room into a wash of white. I squinted and tried to shut my eyes. Had I forgotten to draw the blinds?

Keaton kissed the back of my neck. "Rise and shine, sunshine."

"Mmm, I want to sleep some more."

"No more sleeping. I have fun ways to wake you."

I grumbled. I loved Keaton's wake-up kisses, especially when they were over my clit, but I was just so tired. We'd been up so late for Bastille Day last night. The fact that the man even thought about waking me up right now proved that he was the devil.

The past several months of living in Paris had been like a whirlwind of a dream. We still had a month before I began actual classes for the fall semester, and before Keaton left for England and preseason rugby training. He was still planning on going for a degree in art or design, but after he'd played pro rugby for a few years. Not like he needed the sportsball money, since Keaton Constantine could stand on his feet without it just fine, but simply because he wanted to.

And luckily, this time, he was standing on his feet including me by his side.

There were some people that were just charming, and Keaton was one of them. I asked him the other day what he was more happy about, the rugby deal, or maybe one day opening his own multimedia or design company. He had said both. And then he'd said neither. Then he'd kissed me on the nose and told me that the thing he was most happy about, was having *me*. And that for once, he felt on top of the world. That he could do anything.

He kept kissing me. "*Uhh*, Keaton, I'm tired. I went to bed at two."

"I know. Come on, up you get."

I rolled over reluctantly, but still I rolled over because well, it was Keaton. And the man was magic with his tongue. "Okay fine, convince me."

He laughed, a low rumbling chuckle that made my pussy clench. Okay, he clearly knew definitive ways to do that because now I really was interested.

"Why are you laughing?"

"Because of you, love. Yes, I absolutely would love to wake you up with my mouth on your pussy. But this time, that's not why I'm trying to wake you."

I groaned, irritated. "Then what is so worth getting up for? What time is it?"

He laughed. "It's nine. You've had at least seven hours of sleep."

I was going to kill him. "I hate you."

"No, you love me. But come on, get your lazy ass out of bed."

"Fine. I'm getting my lazy ass out of bed. Why in the world would you wake me up?"

He shook something that sounded like a paper bag, and my nose twitched. He shook it again, and this time my

whole body moved towards the sound and the decadent smell of sugar. "Mmm, is that from La Maison
Pichard?"

"It sure is."

"Give me."

"Tsk, tsk, is that how you ask for things that you want?"

"No, please give me." I reached my hand up blindly,
unwilling to open both eyes.

"You have to try harder than that."

"I'll be your best friend."

"Already are. Try again."

"I will blow you like crazy. Just bring your dick over
here."

His voice went husky. "God, are you serious? You
would blow me for pastries?"

I nodded blindly. I would do anything for a bag of
treats from La Maison Pichard. It was across town. It
was a very tiny bakery, but they had my favorite pain
au chocolat and they made these to-die-for beignets
that they dusted in crack cocaine. Not that I had ever
even seen crack cocaine, but I heard it was addictive, so
that was what it must be. "There is no way you went all

the way to La Maison. But I need them. I will do anything."

He unsnapped his top button, the popping sound making both my eyes open, and I had to blink rapidly to diffuse the light. "Oh really, you'll take the blow job?"

He grinned down at me and rubbed a thumb over my cheek. "I'll always take your mouth on me. Anywhere you want to put it. But if you're offering a blow job, I'm taking it."

Feeling mischievous, I reached for him, slid my hand inside his jeans. When had he gotten dressed? I found him, steely hard and thick and long, and I moaned. What was that thing that made me always want him? That made my core wet and needy, made me desperate for him? I wish I could explain it. I wish I could bottle it. When I pulled him out of his jeans, he groaned. "Jesus fucking Christ, I was kidding. Your hands, they feel so good." He groaned low, moaning.

Feeling excited, I leaned forward—bringing his cock to my lips—lifted my tongue, and licked the head.

He cursed with a little grunt. "Fuck. Fuck. Fuck. Jesus Christ, take it. Take it now."

I snatched the bag out of his hands and continued to lick him. I sucked him in, all the way to the back of my throat. And then there was a knock on our bedroom door.

"Are you two in there boning? It's the last time I bring you pastries from La Maison."

I released him with a loud pop and gasped. "You didn't tell me there were people here."

Keaton held up his hands as his dick bobbed furiously in front of my face. "To be fair, you didn't give me a chance, before you started offering blow jobs, and you know me. I'm completely horned off for you."

"Crap." Then I stopped. Realized something. "Sera, is that you?"

"The one and only, bitch. I mean, how quick can you make that blow job? Because there's shopping to be done."

I glanced right back at Keaton's cock as he was trying to take deep breaths and will it down. "Give me five minutes."

Keaton's brows lifted. "Five? Give me some credit."

I reached for his balls and then licked my lips, and did it again. When his hands fisted in my hair, he groaned. "Okay, fine five. Five minutes."

I pulled back. "Less."

"Woman, you're going to kill me."

"Probably."

Four and a half minutes later, Keaton was laid out on the bed, panting and laughing so hard that I worried for his sanity. I grabbed my bag of goodies, yanked it open, snatched a beignet, then shoved it into my mouth, with no jam or anything—just the powdered sugary goodness, and I moaned.

On the outside of the door, Sera hollered again. "Bitch, you said a blow job, not a full-on sex session. You don't have time for that. Shopping awaits. Come on."

Keaton coughed. "Hey, I do take longer than that in bed."

Sera laughed. "Yeah, *sure* you do. Now come on, Iris. Get a move on, Briggs."

I giggled and scooted out of his reach, but I forgot how fast Keaton was. His hand grabbed my wrist gently and pinned me down. He kissed the powdered sugar off my lips. "I love you, Iris."

I grinned at him. "I love you too, Keaton. Now, if you don't mind, I'm going to go hug my best friend and eat my weight in beignets and pain au chocolat."

He groaned. "Didn't you tell me you were going to be my best friend?"

I shrugged. "That's when you were withholding pastries from me. I would have said anything. Hell, I already *did* do anything to get them."

He groaned. "You know payback is a bitch, right? When I get my hands on you, I'm going to tan that beautiful ass."

"You're welcome to try."

I grabbed a T-shirt and a pair of boxers from the dresser drawer, not caring about dusting the sugar everywhere, or that I probably smelled like orgasms. And then I ran to the door and tugged it open. Sera immediately glanced away. "Lord, make sure the man is dressed. I don't need to see all that." She paused. "Unless the rumors are true and he really is hung like a—"

From inside the bedroom, Keaton cut her off, "Oh, but you'd be lucky to see it."

Sera came right back with a, "I've seen better."

Keaton just snorted a laugh. "I know exactly who it is you see in bed and you wish."

The two of them had learned to bicker properly. "Come on, the gang is all here. We were waiting for you to wake up."

I laughed with sheer, surprised happiness when she dragged me out towards the living room and found our friends. My friends, Keaton's friends. "Holy shit, what are you all doing here?"

There were hugs and kisses all around, and then Keaton came back out from the bedroom, wrapping his arms around my waist. "Happy birthday, love. Your parents will be here tonight, but I figured you would want to celebrate with our friends."

My parents still hadn't gotten used to the idea of Keaton, but they were warming up. And my mother had said that as long as I loved him, she could love him. But if he broke my heart again, she was going to slaughter him.

I turned in his arms, snuggling in the warmth. "I love you so much."

"I know. I love you too."

I looped my arms around his neck and pressed my body to him, and everyone in the room made gagging noises and groaned. But I didn't care. I had Keaton who I'd always wanted, and my freedom. And I had my freedom *my* way.

"So what do you say? A day in Paris with our friends?"

"I couldn't ask for anything more."

The Hellfire Club is just getting heated up. **Callous Prince** is Becker Gray's next Midnight Dynasty release. Art theft, royalty, and enemies-to-lovers make Callous Prince a devious and delicious romance. Order it now.

WANT MORE MIDNIGHT DYNASTY?

Heartless by Jade West

He's *obsessed* with her.

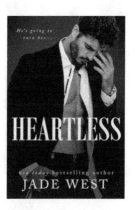

Stroke of Midnight by K. Webster

She's his maid. He's her downfall.

Dark Fairy Tales Anthology

Read the USA Today Bestseller that kicks off Midnight Dynasty.

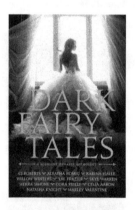

Midnight Dynasty is a brand new world where enemies and lovers are often one and the same.

JOIN THE FACEBOOK GROUP

FOLLOW US ON INSTAGRAM

SIGN UP FOR THE NEWSLETTER

CPSIA information can be obtained
at www.ICGtesting.com
Printed in the USA
FSHW010331101120